The Abbey Mysteries

The Scarlet Spring

Other books in the series

The Buried Cross
The Silent Man
The Drowned Sword

The Abbey Mysteries
The Scarlet Spring

Cherith Baldry

OXFORD
UNIVERSITY PRESS

OXFORD
UNIVERSITY PRESS

Great Clarendon Street, Oxford OX2 6DP

Oxford University Press is a department of the University of Oxford.
It furthers the University's objective of excellence in research,
scholarship, and education by publishing worldwide in

Oxford New York

Auckland Bangkok Buenos Aires Cape Town
Chennai Dar es Salaam Delhi Hong Kong Istanbul Karachi
Kolkata Kuala Lumpur Madrid Melbourne Mexico City Mumbai
Nairobi São Paulo Shanghai Taipei Tokyo Toronto

Oxford is a registered trade mark of Oxford University Press
in the UK and in certain other countries

British Library Cataloguing in Publication Data available

ISBN 0 19 275364 9

1 3 5 7 9 10 8 6 4 2

Printed in Great Britain by
Cox & Wyman Ltd, Reading, Berkshire

Cast of Characters

In the village:

Geoffrey Mason, innkeeper of the Crown in Glastonbury

Idony, his wife

Gwyneth, their daughter

Hereward, their son

Owen Mason, Geoffrey's brother, a stonemason at work on the abbey

Anne Mason, his wife

Matt Green, a stonemason

Finn Thorson, the local sheriff

Ivo and Amabel, their twin children, friends of Gwyneth and Hereward

Rhys Freeman, the local shopkeeper

Tom Smith, the local smith

Hywel, his brother

Dickon Carver, the local carpenter

Margery Carver, his wife

Mistress Flax, a weaver

Wat and Hankin, brothers, servants at the Crown

At the Abbey:
Henry de Sully, abbot of Glastonbury Abbey
Brother Barnabas, the abbey steward
Brother Padraig, the abbey infirmarian
Brother Timothy, a young monk
Brother Peter, an old monk

Visitors to Glastonbury:
Godfrey de Massard, a priest from Wells Cathedral
Marion le Fevre, an embroideress, come to work
    on the abbey's vestments
Ursus, a hermit living on Glastonbury Tor
Nathaniel de Bere, a rich merchant from London
Isabelle Carfax, a lady from Wells
Bernard, her cook

In Wells:
Wasim Kharab, a Moorish merchant
Osbert Teller, his assistant, a dwarf

Glastonbury, south-west England,
AD 1190

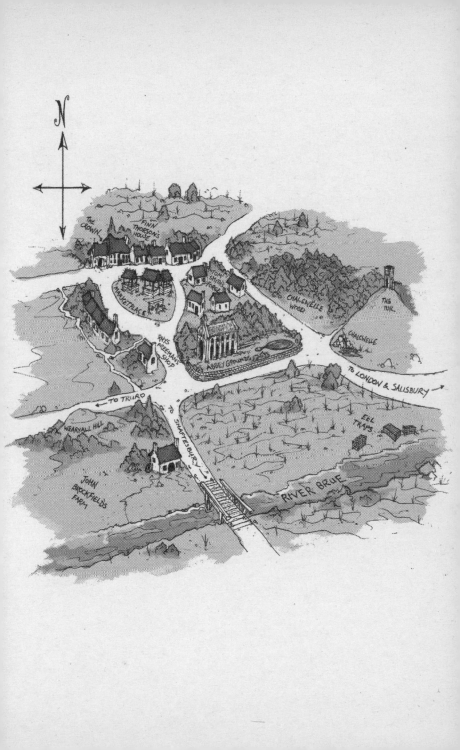

Chapter One

The sun had barely risen and the smoke of hearth fires spiralled upwards from only a handful of houses as Gwyneth and Hereward Mason made their way towards Glastonbury Abbey. They were taking breakfast for the stonemasons from the Crown Inn, where their father was innkeeper. The cold November wind whistled around them and sent dead leaves scuttling against the abbey wall. The street was deserted except for an old, stooped man pushing a handcart containing a few sticks of firewood; he appeared from the abbey gateway and headed off in the direction of the market-place, the iron wheels of his cart rattling on the cobbles in the early morning silence.

Shadows lay thickly under the archway that led into the abbey grounds. As Gwyneth reached the massive stone arch, a hooded monk loomed up out of the darkness, almost knocking the laden basket from her hands. She stepped back, startled, and banged her head against the wall. Blinking away tears of pain, she caught a glimpse of a black-clad figure outlined against the light before the monk vanished into the street.

'Well!' she breathed out crossly, rubbing her head.

Her brother Hereward had flattened himself against the wall outside as the monk rushed by. Glancing after him, he joined Gwyneth under the arch.

'Did you see who that was?' Gwyneth asked.

'Brother Peter,' Hereward replied. 'Going somewhere in a hurry, by the looks of it.'

Gwyneth frowned. Brother Peter was too old and frail to be out of the abbey on such a cold morning. His errand must be urgent indeed. Shrugging, she hauled her basket through the gate and across the precinct to where the stonemasons were at work on the new abbey church. Hereward followed, his back bent under the weight of two heavy skins of ale. The sound of hammers and chisels died away as the men downed tools hungrily and came over to collect their breakfast of ale and bread.

The winter sun stretched pale yellow fingers

over the walls of the half-built church, making the frosty stones glitter. Gwyneth watched her breath puff out into the cold air and imagined how magnificent the building would be when it was finished, more splendid even than before the terrible fire that had destroyed it six years ago. *Not long now*, she thought hopefully, now that the village was prosperous again and there was money to buy materials and pay the wages of the workmen.

The stonemasons clustered eagerly round Hereward so that he could pour ale into their horn beakers. To drive off the winter cold, his father had mulled the ale with spices; the men wrapped grateful fingers round their beakers and ducked their heads to sniff the fragrant steam.

Gwyneth set down her basket of bread on a nearby wall: loaves fresh from the oven, wrapped in linen cloths to keep in the warmth. She began to hand them out, smiling at her Uncle Owen as he came over with a beaker of ale in his hand.

He took the loaf Gwyneth held out to him and bit into it, chewing appreciatively. 'That's better,' he said, swallowing. 'Your mother's bread is the best in Glastonbury. No—the best in England, I'll warrant.'

His praise warmed Gwyneth as much as a hot breakfast. 'I'll make sure to tell her,' she said.

The hideous sound of choking made her break off with a gasp. She spun round and saw Matt Green, another of the stonemasons, drop his empty beaker and clutch at his throat with both hands, staggering about as if he was going to collapse. Hereward was watching, his hazel eyes round with horror as ale trickled out onto the grass from the skin he held.

Gwyneth felt more than the winter cold run through her veins. What could be in the ale, to make Master Green so ill? 'Fetch Brother Padraig!' she exclaimed. 'He's been poisoned!'

Then she realized that some of the other stonemasons had burst into loud guffaws.

'Have done, Matt,' said Owen Mason calmly. 'It's not time yet for the Christmas mumming play. You're frightening the children.'

Matt Green stopped in mid-stagger and let go of his throat, straightening up with a sheepish grin on his face. 'I meant no harm,' he replied. 'I was only remembering how Dean Alexander nearly got himself poisoned last Michaelmas.'

'Dean Alexander!' Gwyneth echoed. She had never seen the powerful cleric, but all Glastonbury knew who he was: the dean of Wells Cathedral, who would like nothing better than to bring Glastonbury Abbey under his rule. He had even sent one of his priests, Godfrey de Massard, here to Abbot Henry— supposedly to deliver letters, but his visit had lasted several weeks already, which made Hereward and Gwyneth quite certain that he was spying on affairs at the abbey for Dean Alexander.

Hereward came over, fastening up the half-empty skin of ale so no more would spill. His face was alive with curiosity. 'I never heard about any poisoning, Master Green. What happened?'

'Well now . . .' Matt Green retrieved his beaker from the ground where he had dropped it. 'There wouldn't be the chance of another mouthful of ale, would there? Tale-telling's thirsty work.'

Half laughing, half exasperated, Hereward poured more ale for Master Green. Gwyneth perched on the wall next to her basket. She blew on her cold fingers and thrust them deep into her cloak, drawing the woollen folds more closely

7

around her as she prepared to listen to the story. Uncle Owen leant against the wall beside her, pulling lumps of bread off his loaf and stuffing them into his mouth.

'This was the way of it,' Matt Green began, once he had taken a gulp of ale. 'Dean Alexander held a great feast two months ago, at Michaelmas. Bishop FitzJocelin from Bath was a guest, and so was Father Aidan, who's said to be the favourite priest of King Richard himself. I heard tell they slaughtered a hundred deer and five hundred chickens for the feast, and bought up all the spices in Wells market-place.'

Just what she would have expected from the priests at Wells, thought Gwyneth. Everyone knew how richly they lived, unlike the devout poverty maintained by the monks at Glastonbury. Dean Alexander feasted as if he were a nobleman, not a man of God.

'The dean's cook had prepared venison,' Master Green went on, 'that being one of Dean Alexander's favourite dishes. And it just so happened that one of the dean's hunting dogs got into the kitchen, and ate the venison from the serving dish that was waiting to go up to the hall.'

He paused to glance round at his audience,

eyes gleaming as he made them wait for the next part of his tale.

'Go on,' Hereward prompted.

'Well, then,' Matt Green continued, 'the next thing anyone knew, the dog was foaming at the mouth and scrabbling with its paws in agony. Before they could do anything, it was dead. The meat had been poisoned! Just think what would have happened if that venison had been served up to the dean and his guests on the high table. All of them dead, and with them some of the most powerful priests in the land!'

'But that's terrible!' Gwyneth exclaimed. 'Who would do such a thing?'

'No one knows,' Owen Mason put in. 'From what I heard, Dean Alexander thought it might have been a mistake in the kitchen, and he sent his cook packing. They say the man was lucky not to be hanged.'

'That's stupid,' said Hereward, down-to-earth as always. 'They wouldn't keep poison in the kitchen, would they?' He gave Gwyneth a side-long glance, his eyes suddenly alight. 'Maybe it was a plot of Henry of Truro?' he suggested. 'I'll wager Father Godfrey thinks so.'

Henry of Truro was the cousin of King

Richard, and he had already made one attempt to assassinate the king. King Richard had pardoned him and sent him into exile in Wales, but since Richard's departure for the Holy Land there were rumours that Henry was plotting once again.

'What good would it do Henry to murder Dean Alexander and his guests?' Gwyneth asked. 'That wouldn't help him become king.'

Hereward grinned. 'Try telling that to Father Godfrey.'

'Well,' said Uncle Owen, brushing crumbs from the front of his tunic, 'storytelling won't get the stone carved. Come on, you lot, let's get back to work.'

Matt Green looked as if he would rather have spent his time drinking ale and gossiping than chipping away with a chisel in this freezing weather, but he set his beaker down and followed Uncle Owen across the site to the blocks of unworked stone. The other masons, too, swallowed their last mouthfuls and returned to their labour. Gwyneth folded the linen cloths into her basket while Hereward went to fetch the other empty ale skin. Waving farewell to their uncle, they walked back through the abbey gate and along the street towards the Crown.

'I wonder what really happened at Wells,' Gwyneth said. 'Do you think Dean Alexander has an enemy?'

Hereward grinned at her. 'Just a few. Almost any of the monks here in Glastonbury, for a start.'

Gwyneth was shocked. 'Hereward, they're holy men!'

'Well, everyone knows that Dean Alexander wants Glastonbury for himself,' said Hereward.

He quickened his pace and Gwyneth hurried to catch up with him. They skirted the stalls in the market-place and waved to Mistress Flax, the linen-weaver, one of the few villagers to brave the cold weather this early in the day.

'I suppose a powerful man like Dean Alexander has lots of enemies,' Gwyneth went on. 'It wouldn't be hard to poison a dish at one of his feasts. There would be so much spice and rich sauce, no one would notice the taste.'

'That's true enough,' Hereward admitted. 'And it looks as if the murderer got away with it. If they had any idea who did it, he would have been arrested by now.'

Gwyneth knew he was right. She and Hereward had discovered the truth about more than one mystery that had troubled the village, but they were unlikely to find out who had tried to poison the dean of Wells and his guests.

Arriving back at the Crown, they were crossing the inn yard when the door opened and their father appeared. He looked around the yard, a baffled expression on his face. 'Have you seen Master de Bere?' he asked as Gwyneth and Hereward came up to him.

Gwyneth shook her head, and Hereward replied, 'No. He wouldn't be out this early, would he?'

'I don't know about that,' said Geoffrey Mason, sounding harassed. 'His bed's been made and the covers are cold, so he's obviously been gone a while.'

Gwyneth exchanged a mystified glance with her brother. Nathaniel de Bere was a rich merchant from London. He had come to Glastonbury two days before on a pilgrimage, to see the recently discovered bones of King Arthur which were now on display at the abbey. After that he had stayed on, telling Geoffrey and Idony Mason that he was interested in the

Tor, and meant to examine the terraces carved out by the priests of the old peoples who had once lived here. Hereward thought he was mad, but Gwyneth could well understand Master de Bere's fascination with the Tor and the legends that enshrouded it. She glanced over her shoulder at the frost-silvered shape of the mysterious hill, its outline blurred by the early morning mist.

'Perhaps he climbed the Tor to see the sun rise,' she suggested.

'Or maybe he sneaked off without paying his bill,' Hereward put in.

Geoffrey Mason shook his head. 'I thought so at first, but his belongings are still in his room and his horse is in the stable.'

'Then maybe someone is holding him for ransom.' Hereward winked at Gwyneth. 'Lord Robert Hardwycke hasn't been visiting, has he?'

'That's not fair!' Gwyneth warned her brother, remembering the uproar in the village when Lord Robert had stolen Eleanor FitzStephen in a mistaken attempt to find the cure for his son's falling sickness. 'Lord Robert knows how wrong he was.'

'He's not held for ransom,' Geoffrey Mason

13

said, irritably brushing away his son's suggestion. 'It's my belief the fool has gone clambering about on the Tor and had some sort of accident. Caught his foot in a rabbit hole, as like as not.' He let out a snort of contempt. 'If he's ruined that furred cloak and his fancy gold-laced boots in the Glastonbury mud, it's no more than he deserves.'

Gwyneth knew that what her father suggested was all too possible. The paths through the woods were treacherous enough for people who knew them well. 'We'll go and look for him,' she offered immediately.

'I'd be glad if you would,' said her father. 'I've got enough to do here. Be back by terce, and if he hasn't turned up by then I suppose I'll have to go and tell Sheriff Thorson.'

Leaving the basket and ale skins by the door to the kitchen, Gwyneth and Hereward went into the street again. By now the village was beginning to wake up. The abbey bell was ringing for the service of nones, and Dickon Carver had joined Mistress Flax in the market-place and was setting up his stall. His wife Margery had begun to unpack wooden bowls from a sack, while a few of the villagers milled between the stalls with their empty baskets.

Further along the road past the abbey, Rhys Freeman unfastened the front door of his shop and stepped out in time to give Gwyneth and Hereward an unfriendly glare as they walked past. He had never been on good terms with them, and he disliked them even more since they had proved that he had stolen the bones of King Arthur from the abbey, and put a stop to his trade in fake relics.

Gwyneth and Hereward did not waste time asking if any of the villagers had seen Nathaniel de Bere. Most of them would not know him, and would have little patience with a visitor who had strayed outside the village before dawn. They hurried on until they left the last houses of the village behind, and the lane dwindled into a narrow track between thickets of hazel and bramble. The huge shape of the Tor, clearly visible now against a pale blue sky, loomed up on their right, and the path began to climb to the left up the gentler slope of Chalcehill. Gwyneth peered from side to side, trying to see if the Crown's missing guest might be anywhere close to the path.

'Master de Bere! Master de Bere!' Hereward called.

The only reply was a beating of wings as three or four birds fluttered up from the undergrowth at the sound of his voice.

'Master de Bere!' Hereward called again. Turning to Gwyneth he said, 'I really don't think he's here. Come on, let's go back.'

Gwyneth grabbed his arm. 'Quiet—I thought I heard something.'

Listening, she heard it again: the crackling sound of someone walking over fallen leaves, crisp with frost. 'Over here!' she exclaimed, darting away from the path and around a massive oak tree.

She was just in time to catch a glimpse of a tall man striding away through the trees—a familiar figure dressed in a brown habit, with a wooden staff in his hand.

'Ursus!' she cried out. 'Ursus, wait!'

Picking up her skirt, she started to run after him, but she had only gone a few paces when her toe jammed against a concealed root and she stumbled forward. She only just saved herself from falling, and by the time she looked up the figure had vanished.

'Was that Ursus?' Hereward asked, catching her up.

Gwyneth nodded. Ursus was a hermit who lived on the slopes of Glastonbury Tor. 'Why didn't he wait?' she said crossly, reaching down to rub her foot. 'We could have asked him if he had seen Master de Bere.'

Hereward shrugged. 'You know what Ursus is like. If he had anything useful to tell us, he would have waited. And if he'd found Master de Bere lying injured, he would have helped him back to the village.'

Gwyneth spent a moment longer staring after the hermit. 'You're right. Let's go on.'

As they retraced their way to the path, they had to leap across a chattering stream, the water a distinctive shade of red as it flowed swiftly through withered clumps of ferns and grasses.

'Chalcwelle!' Gwyneth exclaimed, thinking of the spring where the stream flowed out of the hillside. 'Do you think Master de Bere might have gone there?'

Hereward nodded. 'He might. That was a sacred spring in the old time. It's the sort of place that would interest him.'

'That's true,' Gwyneth said. 'Pilgrims go there still because of the legend of Joseph of Arimathea.

'Tis rumoured that he buried the Holy Grail there and the stream flows red with the blood of Christ. Just imagine if that was true.'

'Well, no one can deny that the stream flows red,' Hereward agreed. 'But father says it's because of the colour of the earth it flows through. The Holy Grail is just a story.'

Gwyneth said nothing. Even the holy brothers at the abbey believed that Joseph of Arimathea had come to Glastonbury. His staff, planted on Wearyall Hill, had flowered into the first of the Holy Thorn trees that dotted the countryside. More important still, he had brought the cup that Jesus Christ had drunk from at the Last Supper. If the Grail were concealed anywhere, what better place than Glastonbury, where so many legends met and mingled? But Gwyneth knew she could argue for days and be no nearer to convincing Hereward.

Climbing further up the hill, she realized that they had almost reached the source of the spring. The path dwindled to little more than a narrow trail among the rocks and ahead of them the stream poured down a steep slope in a series of tiny waterfalls; above it was a wall of exposed rock, hollowed out into a shallow cave where the spring emerged. An eerie silence filled the air; not even the birds were singing.

Gwyneth was struck again by how red the water was: a true, clear scarlet, bright as blood. A chill crept over her and she found herself staring at a single trickle, creeping around a rock at the very edge of the stream. Surely it had never been so red before?

'Hereward.' Her voice came out as a hoarse whisper.

Her brother had begun to climb the slope ahead of her, using both hands to pull himself up over the moss-covered rocks. He paused and looked back. 'What's the matter?'

'Look! Look at the water.'

Hereward opened his mouth to reply, but no words came. When Gwyneth scrambled up beside him, he met her gaze with fear in his eyes. 'It's not supposed to be that red. That is *blood*.'

Gwyneth looked up. She could just see the crack in the rock face where the spring welled up. Below it was a scatter of boulders, as if part of the rock had fallen away long ago. At first she noticed nothing; then she drew in her breath in a tiny gasp.

A pair of feet stuck out from behind one of the boulders, wearing handsome leather boots with gold lacing. The last time Gwyneth had seen them, they had been on the feet of the missing merchant, Nathaniel de Bere.

Chapter Two

'It's him,' Gwyneth whispered.

Hereward's face went white. He swallowed uncomfortably and said, 'We'd better go back to the village for help.'

'But he might not be dead . . .' Gwyneth let her voice trail off. So much blood was coming down with the stream. There could be no hope that Master de Bere still lived, yet to leave him there without even trying to help him seemed wrong.

'There's nothing we can do by ourselves.' Hereward was starting to recover. 'The quicker we can fetch someone, the better.'

He turned and slid down the slope, back onto the path. Gwyneth followed, ashamed of the relief she felt to be leaving the place where Master de Bere was lying. Then her relief turned to terror and she choked back a cry as a tall, dark figure appeared from behind one of the rocks further down the hill.

Seconds later she recognized the monk's habit and the long, bony face beneath the hood. 'Brother Timothy!' she gasped. 'Thank goodness you're here!'

'Gwyneth? Hereward?' said the young monk. 'What's the matter?'

'Up there.' Gwyneth turned and pointed back towards the source of the stream. From here there was nothing to be seen, and Brother Timothy looked mystified.

'There's someone lying up there,' Hereward explained, his voice uneven. 'We think he's dead.'

Brother Timothy's expression darkened. 'Wait here,' he ordered. 'I'll go and look.'

Gwyneth and Hereward watched as the monk climbed up beside the stream. Gwyneth felt her knees begin to tremble, and sat down heavily on a boulder at the side of the path. She wished with all her heart she had never offered to search for Master de Bere. Beside her, Hereward shuffled his feet in the fallen leaves, his eyes fixed on the ground.

After a few moments, Brother Timothy clambered down again to join them. 'The man is dead,' he reported. 'He has a gash on his head three fingers wide.' Making the sign of the cross, he added, 'May God be merciful to him.'

Gwyneth murmured, 'Amen,' and felt too shy to meet Brother Timothy's pale blue gaze. Somehow he looked different, stronger and more commanding than she was used to, not the friend who used to scrump apples with them before he went into the abbey and took his vows.

'What should we do?' Hereward asked anxiously.

'I will stay here to guard the body,' Brother Timothy replied. 'You must take word to the abbey and ask Brother Padraig to come and examine the man.'

'Then you think he might still be alive?'

Brother Timothy shook his head. 'I think not, but a healer should see him nevertheless. Take word to Sheriff Thorson, too, and ask him to come.'

Gwyneth got up to obey, but as she headed down the path she turned back. 'Brother Timothy . . .' Her voice shook and she took a deep breath before going on. 'What do you think happened?'

The monk hesitated. 'He must have dashed his head on the rocky wall beside the spring and fallen into the stream. It was an accident.'

He paused and then repeated, 'Only an accident.'

Gwyneth was very glad of Hereward's sturdy presence by her side as they hurried back to the village. 'Master de Bere would still be alive if he hadn't gone climbing over the rocks in those fancy boots,' she remarked.

Hereward frowned. 'There's something puzzling me . . . something that's not quite right.'

'What do you mean?' Gwyneth asked.

'I don't know. Something about what Brother Timothy said . . .' He shook his head in frustration. 'Perhaps it will come back to me later.'

As they passed the back gate of the abbey, Hereward paused. 'I'll tell Brother Padraig. You go on to Finn Thorson's.'

Without waiting for his sister to reply, he darted in through the gate. Gwyneth went down the street, past Tom Smith's forge where the clink of hammers came from the workshop, and round the corner to the sheriff's house.

As she approached, Ivo and Amabel Thorson, the sheriff's twin children, dashed out from the garden behind the house and capered around her with their red hair flying.

'Come with us, Gwyneth!' said Amabel,

laughing. 'Ivo has made a plan to lure Mistress Carver's pig away!'

'Stop it!' Gwyneth shouted, giddy with her friends' whirling dance and too upset by what she had seen to have any taste for their jesting. 'I need to see your father.'

The twins halted, staring at her. 'Gwyneth, it's only a pig,' Ivo protested. 'We aren't going to hurt it.'

Gwyneth clenched her fists. 'Ivo, sometimes you are so *stupid*!'

'What's going on?' The house door opened and Finn Thorson appeared, his wild hair brushing the lintel as he stepped through the doorway. 'Gwyneth, are you all right?'

'Master Thorson, there's a dead man up at Chalcwelle!' Gwyneth gasped out.

Finn Thorson strode over to her. 'Is this true?' he demanded, giving his son a hard stare. 'Ivo, this isn't one of your jests?'

Dumbstruck, Ivo shook his head.

'I saw him myself, Master Thorson,' Gwyneth explained. To her shame, hot tears pricked her eyes. 'Brother Timothy examined him. He's up there now, waiting for you and Brother Padraig.'

25

'Very well.' Finn Thorson went back into the house, calling for his men.

Amabel gazed at Gwyneth, round-eyed. 'Sorry,' she said in a subdued voice. 'We didn't realize . . . Is it really true?'

Gwyneth nodded, not wanting to talk about it. To her relief, Hereward appeared at that moment, flushed and panting from running down the street. 'Brother Padraig has gone up there with Father Godfrey,' he reported. 'We'd better get home and tell father there's one guest won't be wanting supper tonight.'

'Father Godfrey?' Gwyneth echoed. 'What does *he* want?'

'Abbot Henry was with Brother Padraig when I spoke to him,' Hereward explained. 'He wanted someone to keep an eye on things on behalf of the abbey, and Father Godfrey offered to go.'

'He'll be looking for another plot of Henry of Truro,' Gwyneth said with a disdainful sniff. 'Well, he'll be disappointed this time. I dare say we must expect more accidents like this, if more pilgrims come who aren't used to walking round here.'

She bade a quick farewell to Ivo and Amabel, and walked with her brother down the street towards the Crown. As soon as they were out of earshot of their friends, Hereward said, 'I've remembered what was bothering me, about what Brother Timothy told us.'

Gwyneth halted. 'What?'

Hereward hesitated before replying, as if he was reluctant to voice what he was thinking. 'He said that Master de Bere must have hit his head against the rock wall. But I couldn't see any blood on the rocks. I know I wasn't there for long, but the rocks were clean and shiny with frost, I'm sure of it.'

'Then perhaps he fell and hit his head on the bottom of the stream.'

'The stream bed is soft silt,' Hereward objected. 'If he had fallen straight into the water, he wouldn't have been stunned enough to drown, and there wouldn't have been all that blood.'

'But if he didn't hit his head on the rocks . . .' Gwyneth began, her throat suddenly dry.

'Then something else must have hit him,' Hereward said grimly. 'Or some*one*.'

Gwyneth turned to her brother, feeling her heart begin to pound. 'Then you're saying that you think Master de Bere was *murdered*?'

Hereward nodded, his mouth tight.

'Then did Brother Timothy lie to us? But he's a holy man!' Slowly Gwyneth crossed the inn yard and sat down on the rim of the well. She hugged herself to keep out the cold, though she knew that nothing would drive off the chill of the thoughts racing through her head. 'What was Brother Timothy doing there?' she wondered out loud, feeling as if every word was being wrenched out of her. 'We heard the bell ringing for nones as we left the village. He should have been in the chapel!'

'You're not thinking—' Hereward broke off, took a breath, and tried again. 'You can't think Brother Timothy had anything to do with Master de Bere's death?'

Gwyneth shook her head miserably. 'I don't know.'

'But he was coming *up* the path when we first saw him,' Hereward pointed out. 'We'd already seen the blood. Master de Bere was dead by then.'

Gwyneth shivered. 'Unless he heard us there and made his way round from the spring to the path, so that we would *think* he had just arrived.' She met Hereward's gaze and saw that he was just as horrified that what she suggested might be true.

'I don't *want* to believe Brother Timothy's a murderer!' she cried. 'But he was there, and he lied to us about the blood on the rock wall.'

'He might not have lied—perhaps he just didn't notice there was no blood on the wall. After all, you didn't. And besides, he's not the only person we saw there.' Hereward's voice was tense with shock, and the look he gave Gwyneth was a challenge. 'Ursus was in the woods too.'

'Ursus!' Gwyneth jumped to her feet again. 'Hereward, no!'

'He was there,' Hereward repeated, 'heading away from the spring.'

Gwyneth felt tears sting her eyes. 'No—we're talking nonsense!' she said. 'Why would Brother Timothy or Ursus want to kill Master de Bere? He only came to Glastonbury two days ago. We don't know that they even met him.'

'He went to the abbey to see Arthur's bones.' Hereward's mouth twisted, as if the last thing he wanted was to find evidence against either of their friends. 'And he was wandering about on the Tor . . . he could have spoken to Ursus there.'

'But we don't *know* he did,' Gwyneth insisted. 'And even if they spoke together, what reason would they have to kill him? Nobody in

Glastonbury would want to kill him,' she went on fiercely. 'He was a stranger. He told father when he arrived that he had never been here before. He must have brought the reason for his murder with him.'

'Have you found him?' Geoffrey Mason's voice interrupted. Gwyneth turned to see her father coming out of the inn and crossing the yard towards them. 'Well?' he asked. 'What news?'

'We think we found him,' Hereward replied quietly.

'What do you mean, you think?'

'There's a man lying dead up at Chalcwelle,' Gwyneth said. 'We didn't see him close to, but he was wearing boots like Master de Bere's.'

'What!' Geoffrey Mason stared in astonishment.

'We told Master Thorson and Brother Padraig,' Hereward went on. 'They went up there.'

His father pushed both hands through his thatch of greying hair. 'I said he would come to no good, wandering around the Tor.'

Hereward opened his mouth to speak and Gwyneth knew that he was going to mention murder. She shot him a warning glance to silence him. For now it was best to let people think that

Master de Bere's death had been an accident, since they had only Hereward's observations about the cave wall to suggest anything otherwise.

'The stream was all red with blood,' she said, shuddering.

'You'd better come inside,' said her father, putting an arm round her shoulders. 'Let's get some hot food into you, and you can tell us everything.'

When they went into the warm kitchen, Idony Mason turned from stirring a pot of oatmeal on the fire, her brows lifting in surprise as she saw them. 'Whatever's the matter?' she asked. 'You're both white as a sheet!'

'It's Master de Bere,' Geoffrey Mason replied heavily. 'They found him dead at Chalcwelle.'

'Dead?' Idony dropped the spoon so that she could hug both her children to her, clucking like an anxious hen. 'And you saw the body? Geoffrey, you had no business sending them out to look for him!'

'I would never have asked them to search had I known what they'd find, my love.' Geoffrey Mason shook his head regretfully. 'Who would have expected this?'

31

Idony gave Gwyneth and Hereward a gentle push towards the kitchen table, before ladling oatmeal into wooden bowls. 'Sit down and tell us what happened.'

Gwyneth sank thankfully onto a stool. It was a relief to sit there, surrounded by the comforting cooking smells, and spoon up the hot oatmeal while she and Hereward repeated the story. Gwyneth kept to the facts of what they had seen, and what Brother Timothy had told them. She did not mention their suspicions that Master de Bere had been murdered, and to her relief Hereward said nothing either. Their mother listened silently, her face pale and shocked.

'We can't be sure it was Master de Bere,' Gwyneth finished. 'But he's still missing, and the dead man—'

'Dead man?' A voice spoke behind Gwyneth and she glanced round to see Marion le Fevre standing in the kitchen doorway. Mistress le Fevre was an embroideress who had come to Glastonbury to make new altar cloths for the abbey; she had been staying at the Crown for some weeks now while she worked.

'Can I get you anything, mistress?' Idony asked, rising to her feet.

'Yes, thank you, some of your delicious camomile tea,' Marion replied, coming further into the room. 'But, Gwyneth, what dead man is this? Surely not more trouble for your poor village?' Her green eyes were huge with anxiety: she was so beautiful, Gwyneth thought, and so readily concerned about Glastonbury's fortunes!

'One of our guests,' said Geoffrey Mason. 'Or at least, so we think.' While Idony withdrew to the fire to make the tea, he quickly explained to Mistress le Fevre what had happened.

'Oh, sweet saints!' Marion exclaimed, pressing one white hand to her forehead. 'How terrible! I saw him only last night at supper.'

Before she could say more, a loud knock sounded on the outer door.

'Enter!' Geoffrey called.

The door opened and Gwyneth's eyes widened in surprise as she recognized the tall, austere figure of Godfrey de Massard, clad in his jet-black habit, with polished rosary beads gleaming at his waist.

'Father Godfrey, be welcome,' said Geoffrey Mason, rising. 'Will you take some wine?'

'No, I thank you.' For once Father Godfrey seemed to lack his usual air of haughty disdain, as if the sight of Master de Bere's body had troubled him too. 'I need information, that is all. You have heard of the dead man at Chalcwelle?'

The innkeeper nodded. 'I fear it is our missing guest, Master Nathaniel de Bere.'

'That is what I have come to ask,' said Father Godfrey. 'The corpse is that of a man of middling height, dark haired, well-fed, with a fleshy face and a hooked nose. He wore a gold ring with a turquoise set into it.'

Idony crossed herself as Geoffrey Mason said heavily, 'That is indeed the man.'

The priest nodded. 'Abbot Henry has asked me to look into the matter on behalf of the abbey,' he went on.

'But what need?' Geoffrey Mason interrupted. He added sadly, 'I should have warned him how dangerous it is to go wandering around on the Tor in the dark. People fall, they drown in the marshes . . .'

'Do not trouble yourself, Master Mason,' said Father Godfrey. 'Nathaniel de Bere did not die accidentally. All the signs indicate that someone killed him.'

Marion le Fevre let out a startled cry. The earthenware mug of tea, which Idony had just handed to her, slipped from her fingers and shattered on the flagstones. Hot liquid splashed everywhere. 'Killed?' she echoed. 'Merciful God, no! We'll all be murdered in our beds.'

Father Godfrey gave her a chilly look; Gwyneth thought it was typical of the hard-hearted priest to be unmoved by the beautiful woman's distress. 'I think not, mistress,' he said. 'The reason for this crime cannot lie in Glastonbury. Master de Bere was a stranger here.'

His words did not seem to reassure Mistress le Fevre. With a muffled sob she fled from the kitchen, leaving Hereward to collect the broken pieces of the mug and Idony to fetch a cloth and wipe up the spilt tea. Gwyneth looked sympathetically after the embroideress, and resolved to take her more tea once Godfrey de Massard had gone.

'She'll leave if we're not careful,' Idony warned, swiping angrily at the wet floor. 'And so will all the other guests. Who would want to come to Glastonbury to be murdered? We'll be ruined!'

'Of your courtesy, Master Mason,' Father Godfrey went on, as if the interruption had not occurred, 'have Master de Bere's belongings packed up and sent to me at the abbey. I must examine them to see if there is anything to tell us why he was killed.'

Geoffrey Mason looked embarrassed. 'Begging your pardon, Father, but . . . well, Master de Bere has not paid his bill. Usually I would expect to keep his things.'

Father Godfrey waved a hand dismissively. 'That is not my concern. I have offered to help Finn Thorson and his orders must come first. I may be able to return some of Master de Bere's possessions when I have finished my investigation.'

Gwyneth could see that her father was not satisfied by the half-promise, but there was nothing more he could say. 'We'll pack the things up,' she suggested. 'And take them up to the abbey.'

Father Godfrey acknowledged her offer with a nod. 'Make sure you pack up every single thing,' he instructed. 'Leave nothing behind. And let me warn you and your brother. You may have helped find out certain truths in the past—' Gwyneth guessed it was difficult for the haughty priest to admit this—'but this is a matter of murder. It is not for children to interfere in.' Giving Gwyneth and Hereward no chance to respond, he added a brief, 'Good day to you,' and swept out of the kitchen.

'Well!' Idony Mason exclaimed, and then added sharply, 'Mind, he's right. You two stay in the village where it's safe.'

'Better do as he asks with Master de Bere's belongings,' said their father. 'I'll wager Father Godfrey won't like to be kept waiting.'

Gwyneth regretted her offer now. The last thing she wanted to do was help Father Godfrey after he had been so unpleasant. But curiosity was pricking her. Why was the priest so keen to see Master de Bere's possessions? Did he expect there to be a reason for his untimely death among them? If she and Hereward packed up the merchant's things, they would have a chance to examine them before Father Godfrey.

She hastily swallowed the last of her oatmeal and led the way upstairs to the bedchamber where Nathaniel de Bere had slept. It was a fine panelled room, the best in the inn except for the one Marion le Fevre was occupying. The merchant had been a wealthy man, well able to afford privacy and comfort.

Master de Bere had not left much behind him. In the clothes chest Gwyneth found a spare tunic and an overmantle of purple velvet trimmed with gold at the neck and hem. There was a pair of soft leather slippers, but no other shoes; she suppressed a shiver as she remembered his fine boots, and where she had last seen them. She rolled the clothes into a bundle and placed them on the bed. 'I can't see what Father Godfrey is going to find out from these,' she said.

'There's no sign of a purse,' added Hereward. 'I was hoping we might find some money, and then father could take what's owed him.'

'I expect Master de Bere had it with him,' said Gwyneth. 'Hereward, suppose he was killed by robbers? A purse of coins would give a desperate man cause for murder.'

'I don't think so,' Hereward replied. 'Don't you remember? Father Godfrey said he was wearing a gold ring with a turquoise. Robbers would have taken that as well as any purse.'

'Yes, you're right.' Gwyneth bent down to pick up a folded undershirt, then turned to see Hereward standing by the window. He was examining an earthenware water flask.

'Is this one of ours?' he asked, flourishing it. 'Or did Master de Bere bring it with him?'

'He must have,' replied Gwyneth. 'I've never seen that kind here.'

'We'd better take it, then,' said her brother. 'Here—catch!'

'Hereward, don't—' Gwyneth was too late; the flask was already flying through the air towards her. She dropped the shirt, but she wasn't quick enough to catch the flask; it hit the floor and broke into several fragments.

'Hereward, how could you be so stupid!' she began, but her voice trailed off as she stared at the shattered flask. Instead of water spilling out, a rolled-up tube of fine linen lay at her feet. Hereward bent down to pick it up. It crackled as he touched it, and he unfolded it to reveal a piece of rolled up parchment. Looking up, he met Gwyneth's gaze.

'Whoever put this into the flask did not intend it to be found, surely?' he said, his voice shaking with excitement. 'Do you think this is it? Have we found the reason Master de Bere was murdered?'

Chapter Three

'It must be important to have been hidden so well,' Gwyneth agreed breathlessly.

She and Hereward sat side by side on the bed while Hereward unrolled the parchment. A second sheet, rolled up inside it, fell out and slid to the floor. Ignoring it for the moment, Gwyneth stared down at the document in Hereward's hands.

It looked very old; the parchment was yellowed and blotched with brown and the edges were ragged. In the top right-hand corner was a symbol roughly drawn in scarlet ink, shaped like a teardrop. The rest of the sheet was covered in lines and lines of writing, the ink faded to a brownish colour that in places was almost indistinguishable from the shade of the parchment. Gwyneth felt a jolt of disappointment when she realized that the letters were completely unfamiliar—strange, swirling shapes with curls and dots above and below the words. She was used to reading her father's accounts and inventories, and Hereward had been taught to read by the monks like the other village boys, but this document defeated both of them.

'We can't read it!' Hereward sounded just as frustrated.

Gwyneth stared fiercely at the writing as if she could will the graceful script to rearrange itself into something she could understand.

'I wonder what that is,' Hereward said after a moment, pointing to the scarlet teardrop.

'It looks like blood,' said Gwyneth, shutting her eyes briefly as she remembered the streams of scarlet flowing down from Chalcwelle.

'Or part of a nobleman's coat of arms,' Hereward suggested. He turned the document over. 'There's no seal.'

There was nothing written on the other side of the sheet. Nothing to tell them why Master de Bere was carrying the document, or why he wanted to keep it so secret that he had hidden it inside the water flask.

Gwyneth remembered the second sheet that had been rolled up inside the first. Bending down, she rescued it from the floor and spread it out on her lap. This document was a small piece of crisp, new parchment, with fewer lines than the first. To Gwyneth's relief it was written in English.

It was addressed to Master Nathaniel de Bere. With a surge of anticipation, Gwyneth began to read aloud. ' "You have asked me for gold, but I am a poor priest and have none. Yet the document that I send you, and the medallion, are more precious than all the gold in Christendom. I pray you be satisfied. If you make known my terrible crime then you will ruin me, and bring Holy Church into disrepute. Daily I pray for your pity and God's forgiveness. I beg you, Master de Bere, take this, the one treasure that I have to give, and trouble me no longer." It's signed, "Father Herbert of Smithfield",' she finished.

Hereward had read the letter along with her, his lips moving silently, and now he looked up at her with his eyes shining. '. . . more precious than all the gold in Christendom,' he echoed. He gazed down at the first document, his brow furrowing. 'What's so precious about it? And what's this about a medallion? I can't see it here.' He shook out the linen wrappings and poked through the scraps of broken pottery, but there was no medallion to be found.

Meanwhile Gwyneth was reading the letter again. 'He talks about a crime . . .' she murmured. 'And Master de Bere had asked him for gold in return for not making his sins known. Hereward, Master de Bere must have been blackmailing the man who wrote this letter, Father Herbert. Perhaps he killed de Bere to keep him quiet!'

Hereward shook his head. 'Smithfield is in London, where Master de Bere came from. If Father Herbert wanted to murder him, he'd hardly come all the way to Glastonbury to do it.'

'That's true.' Gwyneth gestured towards the first document. 'I think we ought to keep this, and the letter,' she said. 'Perhaps we'll be able to find someone who can read it.'

Hereward stared at her. 'Are you mad? If Father Godfrey found out we'd kept hold of them, he would be furious.'

But Gwyneth could not forget the dismissive way Father Godfrey had spoken, nor stop herself from wanting to discover the truth before he did. 'It would serve him right if we found the murderer,' she said stubbornly. 'He's no right to treat us like foolish children. Besides, the parchments were well hidden. Once we've had the chance to investigate, we can find them again, and pass them on to Father Godfrey.'

Hereward shook his head, but Gwyneth could see a gleam beginning to wake in his eyes.

'Just for a day or two,' she added persuasively. 'It can't do any harm. Nothing will bring Master de Bere back.'

'Well . . . all right.' Hereward's curiosity won over his natural caution. He knelt on the floor and began to gather up the broken scraps of earthenware. 'I'll take these to the rubbish heap,' he said. 'As far as we're concerned, there never was a water flask, so there couldn't have been anything hidden inside it!'

'We ought to go up to Chalcwelle again,' said Hereward. He and Gwyneth had just left the abbey after delivering the rest of Nathaniel de Bere's possessions to Father Godfrey. 'We may discover something there that Finn Thorson's men might have missed.'

'I don't know.' Gwyneth felt sick at the thought of their last visit to the scarlet spring. 'Mother told us to stay in the village.'

'She won't know,' Hereward said confidently.

'She excused us from our tasks for the rest of the day, and she'll be too busy with the cooking to wonder where we are.'

Gwyneth wrinkled her brow uncertainly. She was uneasy at the thought of disobeying their mother, especially when there was a murderer loose in the village. 'I hope they've taken Master de Bere's body away,' she said.

'They will have,' Hereward assured her. 'Come on. We've got all afternoon to search. We might be able to see if anyone was lying in wait for him there—or perhaps someone followed him.'

'All right.' Gwyneth was still unconvinced, but she followed her brother along the street and up the track that led to Chalcwelle. There were signs that more feet had trampled along it since the early morning: Finn Thorson and his men, Gwyneth guessed, or perhaps some of the more curious villagers.

When they reached the slope where the stream spilled down to join the path, she was relieved to see that the water had recovered its faint rusty tinge; the bright scarlet of Master de Bere's blood had vanished. A voice hailed them as they began to climb, and when they reached the top of the slope they saw Tom Smith's brother Hywel standing beside the cave where the spring poured out.

'Were you looking for Master Thorson?' he asked. 'He's not here. He and his men took the body away.' His blue eyes shone earnestly as he added, 'He told me to stay and keep an eye on things until he could come back to have a proper look round.'

'Do you know what happened here, Hywel?' asked Gwyneth. 'Did Master Thorson say anything before he took the body away?'

Hywel Smith seemed to swell with importance. 'I'll show you. Come and look here.'

Gwyneth and Hereward went to join him by the spring. Above the cave, the rock stretched sheer above their heads. Bright green ferns and grasses had rooted themselves in cracks here and there, and halfway up the wall of the cave, the water of Chalcwelle poured out in a smooth curve to fall into a bubbling pool. The stream flowed out of the cave and ran across a narrow stretch of level ground, until it spilled down the slope towards the track.

'He was lying just there,' said Hywel, pointing to a patch of flattened grass. 'His head was in the stream there, just where it leaves the pool. And look here,' he went on eagerly, beckoning.

Gwyneth and Hereward followed him beside the wall for a few paces until they came to a spot where the ground had been churned up, with marks of booted feet pressed into the mud.

'There must have been a fight,' said Hereward, squatting down to examine the marks more closely. 'There are two different footprints here.'

'Don't touch them,' Hywel said anxiously. 'Master Thorson said most particularly not to touch anything.'

'That's all right, we won't,' Gwyneth reassured him with a smile.

As Hywel beckoned them further, they saw that the footprints ended in a mound of earth, thrown up from a hole in the ground. A horn lantern lay beside it.

'Did Master de Bere dig this?' Hereward asked. 'I can't see a spade.'

'Master Thorson took the spade with him.' Hywel's voice grew hushed as he added, 'It was lying by the pool. Master Thorson reckons it was the spade that killed him.'

Gwyneth's stomach lurched as she imagined an iron spade smashing down on Master de

Bere's head. To distract herself, she peered down into the hole. 'I wonder what he was digging for, before dawn?'

'Maybe he thought there was treasure buried here,' Hereward suggested.

He bent over the hole to take a closer look, and Gwyneth heard his tiny intake of breath. Cautiously, so that Hywel would not see, he pointed, and Gwyneth saw the tiny glint of something metal, half covered by loose soil. Hereward's eyes were gleaming, but Hywel had told them not to touch.

Gwyneth straightened up. 'Is that Master Thorson coming back?' she asked, as if she heard sounds from the track below.

Hywel snapped to attention and walked a few paces towards the slope, from where he could see the path. Instantly Hereward swooped down, grabbed the shiny object from the hole and stood up again in time to meet Hywel with an innocent look as he turned back.

'I don't reckon so,' Hywel said. His broad, wind-reddened face was earnest and trusting. 'Perhaps you heard a fox.'

'Yes, I must have done,' Gwyneth agreed with a twinge of conscience.

'We should be going,' Hereward said. 'Goodbye, Hywel.'

'Goodbye,' Hywel replied, trudging back to take up his place by the spring.

Gwyneth and Hereward clambered down the slope and took the track towards the village. As soon as they rounded the first corner Gwyneth whispered, 'Show me what was in the hole!'

Hereward stopped walking and unfolded his fist. Lying on the palm of his hand was something small and metallic, covered in sticky soil. Gwyneth picked it up and rubbed off the earth to reveal a tiny copper medallion in the shape of a teardrop. A hole was pierced through it with a ring of copper wire so it could be hung from a chain. One side of it was enamelled in bright scarlet so that it glowed like a drop of blood in the winter sunlight.

'It's a medallion!' Hereward breathed. 'Like the drawing on the parchment. This must be what Father Herbert sent to Nathaniel de Bere!'

'And Master de Bere dropped it in the hole while he was struggling with his murderer,' Gwyneth added. 'But what does it mean? Father Herbert said it was precious, but there's nothing to tell us why!'

49

'Or to tell us who killed Master de Bere,' Hereward said.

Gwyneth rubbed one forefinger over the enamel. 'Perhaps the murderer wanted this?' she suggested. 'He killed Master de Bere for it, and searched the body not realizing that Master de Bere had dropped it.'

'But *why*?' Hereward sounded baffled. 'It's too small to be valuable, even if it were made of gold. There must be something else important about it, but how do we find out what?'

'There might be one way,' said Gwyneth. 'Ursus might be able to tell us. He knows all kinds of things. We could show him the parchment, too.'

Hereward frowned. 'But Ursus was here when we found the body,' he reminded his sister. 'He might have killed Master de Bere himself.' Ignoring Gwyneth's instinctive protest, he went on, 'And if he did, then taking the parchment and the medallion to him would be the stupidest thing we could do.'

Gwyneth thought about the hermit, the wisdom of his words and the kindness in his blue eyes. The idea of him being a brutal murderer wrenched at her heart; if that was true, then so much that she had believed was nothing more than a lie. Slowly, meeting Hereward's gaze, she said, 'You don't really believe that.'

Hereward hesitated. 'I don't *want* to believe it.' Then he nodded. 'All right. We'll show him. But if he wants to take us down any more holes in the Tor, I'm not going!'

As he spoke, they heard the distant sound of several people tramping up the path, and the baying of hunting dogs. Finn Thorson's voice drifted through the trees as he gave an order to his men. Gwyneth and Hereward looked at each other, and in unspoken agreement they plunged off the track and into the woods.

Gwyneth and Hereward had never discovered where abouts on the Tor Ursus had his cell. Gwyneth imagined a cave with the entrance screened by brambles, or perhaps a hut built from rough blocks of stone mortared with mud from the river. She respected the hermit's desire to live in seclusion, yet now, filled with anxiety, she wished she knew a place where she could be sure of finding him.

They skirted the lower slopes of the Tor,

heading towards the river where they had found Ursus before. The marshy ground was harder now in the winter frosts. Ice fringed the pools of still water, the dead stems of reeds poking through it. Silvery icicles hung glittering from the branches of trees.

As they came within sound of the river, Hereward stopped and called out, 'Ursus! Ursus, where are you?'

There was no reply, but a moment later he and Gwyneth rounded a thicket of hazel saplings to see the hermit standing on the river bank with his back to them. He held a spear poised over the water; as Gwyneth watched he stabbed it down and drew it up again with a fish wriggling on the point.

'Ursus!' Gwyneth exclaimed, hurrying towards him. 'I'm so glad we've found you!'

Ursus turned, his blue eyes lighting up with a smile of welcome. Surely, Gwyneth thought, a murderer could not look so friendly?

'I am here,' he said simply, pulling the fish off the end of the spear and tossing it into a basket where two or three others lay. 'What is your need of me?' He thrust the spear into the soft ground at the edge of the river—it was made of a length of ashwood, Gwyneth saw, with a point of sharpened flint bound to it with twine—and sat on a nearby rock.

Hereward brought out the documents from his pouch and held out the parchment with the unfamiliar writing. 'We wondered what you can tell us about this,' he said.

Ursus took the parchment in his strong, long-fingered hands. As soon as he glanced at it his eyebrows rose in astonishment and for a moment he scarcely seemed to breathe. 'Where did you get this?'

Gwyneth felt a quiver of excitement; Ursus clearly recognized the document and would be able to tell them something about it. 'It belonged to a guest at the Crown.' She quickly explained who Nathaniel de Bere was, and how they had discovered his body at Chalcwelle.

'The parchment was hidden in a water flask in his room,' Hereward added. 'This was with it, too.' He handed Ursus the letter from Father Herbert.

The hermit's expression darkened as he read it. 'This is a plot of wicked men,' he said. 'It may be that Master de Bere was involved in great evil.'

'But the parchment,' Gwyneth prompted him. 'What does it mean? Can you read it?'

Ursus glanced down at the parchment again. The flash of amazement when he first saw it was hidden now, and his voice was expressionless as he said, 'No, I cannot. And I doubt that it has any bearing on Master de Bere's death.'

'What?' Gwyneth knew she sounded rude, but she couldn't imagine how Ursus could say such a thing after the way the document had been hidden so carefully with the letter from Father Herbert.

Ursus calmly met her gaze. 'A document about Glastonbury would be written in English or Latin. This is Arabic. A London merchant would be unable to read it.'

'But I know who could!' Hereward leapt up as if he wanted to dash off then and there. 'Wasim Kharab!'

Gwyneth felt her heart begin to beat faster. In the autumn just past, they had met a Moorish merchant named Wasim Kharab who had been involved with the shopkeeper Rhys Freeman in an operation to sell fake holy relics. According to Godfrey de Massard, Wasim was raising money to help Henry of Truro. Hereward was right that he would be able to read the parchment, but he could be a dangerous man to seek out. Besides, Gwyneth thought, her brief flash of excitement fading, Wasim travelled far and might be anywhere by now. The chances of him coming back to Glastonbury, after the fake relics had been exposed, were faint indeed.

Ursus waved away Hereward's suggestion. 'Perhaps the merchant could read it for you, but I still believe it would prove to be of little importance.'

'Then what about this?' Hereward persisted. He scrabbled in his pouch and brought out the copper teardrop. 'Father Herbert's letter speaks of a medallion, and we found this in the hole Master de Bere was digging at Chalcwelle.'

'He was digging?' Ursus's voice had grown sharper again.

'Someone had dug a hole there,' Gwyneth told him. 'We think it must have been Master de Bere.'

Ursus studied the medallion, the scarlet enamel making it look like a gash in the palm of his hand. 'This tells you nothing,' he said discouragingly, 'except that Master de Bere had it with him when he died.' He closed his fingers on the medallion; briefly Gwyneth thought that he looked as if he wanted to keep it, and the parchment as well.

'What are you going to do?' she asked nervously.

Ursus let out a long sigh. 'I will do nothing,' he said. 'It is not my part to meddle in these affairs. And I advise you to do nothing, too.' He rose from the rock. For a moment he had an imperious look about him that reminded Gwyneth of Father Godfrey. He handed the medallion back to Hereward and gave the parchment and the letter to Gwyneth. 'Take these to your sheriff,' he ordered. 'Much blood has been spilled over secrets like these, as Nathaniel de Bere discovered to his cost. It would grieve me if any such harm came to you.'

Chapter Four

Hereward slept badly that night. His dreams were filled with images of Nathaniel de Bere's body at Chalcwelle and the stream flowing scarlet with spilled blood. Next morning when he rose and went down to the kitchen with Gwyneth, he half expected some faceless figure to leap out at them from the shadows at the turn of the stairs.

He was unprepared for the pungent smell that hit him in the throat and made his eyes water when he opened the kitchen door. Inside the smell was stronger still; aromatic fumes rose from a small pot that his mother was stirring on the fire.

'There you are, Hereward,' said Idony as he came in. 'I was just going to wake you. This is finished, so you can take some up to the abbey for me.'

'What on earth is it?' Gwyneth asked, coughing as she followed Hereward into the kitchen.

'Brother Padraig gave me a receipt for an ointment to cure chilblains,' Idony Mason explained as she drew the pot off the fire. 'You know how everybody suffers from them when the weather gets cold, and I like to keep some on hand for the guests—if we have any guests left after this terrible murder. I said I'd make a batch and share it with Brother Padraig, to save him the trouble.'

She took down some small earthenware jars from a shelf and began to fill them with the sticky ointment. Hereward opened the door to the inn yard to let some of the fumes out.

'I'll go with Hereward,' Gwyneth offered, fetching a basket.

'No, I need you to help me here,' said her mother. 'You know you won't be allowed into the infirmary.'

Gwyneth made a face behind her mother's back. 'See if you can find out anything,' she whispered to Hereward. 'Ask whether a priest from London has been staying in the guesthouse.'

That would be easier said than done, Hereward reflected as he trudged up the street towards the abbey, munching on one of his mother's warm loaves. It was none of his business who stayed in the abbey guesthouse.

As he entered the precinct, he saw his Uncle Owen talking to Matt Green; his uncle raised a hand in greeting but did not come over to speak to him. None of the monks were outside, so Hereward hurried past the half-built church and across the snow-covered turf to the infirmary.

When he put his head round the door he could not see Brother Padraig. The infirmary was a long, low room, with whitewashed walls and rows of small beds on either side. At the far end was a door that led to a storeroom. Hereward saw Brother Peter in the bed nearest the door, his frail body shaken by a fit of coughing. Hereward guessed he was paying the price for his early morning errand the day before. Brother Timothy was sitting beside the old man, speaking to him in a low voice.

Hereward stepped forward. 'Brother Timothy . . .' he began hesitantly, remembering his and Gwyneth's suspicions of the young monk.

Brother Timothy looked up. 'Shut the door,' he snapped. 'Can't you feel the draught?'

Hereward murmured, 'Your pardon, Brother,' as he closed the door behind him. He was sure he wasn't imagining the change in Brother Timothy, despite the pricking of his conscience.

The young monk's friendliness had vanished, replaced with an irritable air that would have done credit to Father Godfrey himself.

'What do you want?' Brother Timothy demanded.

'I'm looking for Brother Padraig.'

Brother Timothy jerked his head towards the far end of the infirmary. 'In the storeroom.'

Hereward thanked him, casting a nervous glance at him as he passed. There seemed no good reason for Brother Timothy's behaviour; he could not possibly know that Hereward and Gwyneth suspected him of Master de Bere's murder. Unless he truly was guilty . . .

Brother Peter's coughing interrupted his thoughts. 'Such grievous sin,' he heard the old man say. 'I shall never be clean of it.'

'Don't speak so,' Brother Timothy murmured, his voice instantly gentle.

Hereward lost whatever else he might have said as the storeroom door opened and Brother Padraig came out, closely followed by Godfrey de Massard. The priest looked pale and drawn, with dark circles around his eyes.

'. . . infuse them in water for the time it takes you to say a Paternoster,' Brother Padraig was saying to Father Godfrey, handing him a packet of herbs. 'Then drink the infusion and your headache will surely be cured.'

'Thank you, Brother,' said the priest. He swept past Hereward with a curt nod and left the infirmary.

Brother Padraig turned to Hereward, smiling. 'What can I do for you?'

Hereward held out the basket. 'My mother sent this, Brother. It's the chilblain ointment.'

'Excellent!' Brother Padraig's smile grew broader as he took the basket from Hereward. 'Wait there while I put the jars away, and you may carry your mother's basket back.'

He returned to the storeroom; Hereward stood very still, aware of the low-voiced conversation between Brother Peter and Brother Timothy, but unable to make out the words.

He noticed a faint glint on the floor on the other side of the room, and without really thinking he went over to it. Something small and metallic was lodged between two of the floor-boards. Hereward stooped down to prise it up, and could not suppress a gasp when he saw that he was holding a copper teardrop enamelled in scarlet.

His first thought was that he had dropped the one he had found at Chalcwelle, but when he squeezed his pouch he could feel its hard outline through the leather. So here was a second one!

'What's that you have there, Hereward?'

He straightened up with a jump to see Brother Timothy standing just behind him. He took a deep breath and forced himself to speak normally. 'Only this. Do you know what it is?' He held out the teardrop on the palm of his hand, without taking his eyes off Brother Timothy's face. Would the monk betray his guilt at the sight of the medallion?

Something flashed in Brother Timothy's eyes. 'A mere trifle, nothing more . . .' He picked it up and examined it. 'It appears to have little value.'

'You don't know who it belongs to?' Hereward pressed.

'It is hardly something that a holy brother would possess,' Brother Timothy pointed out. 'But I will make enquiries.'

He returned to Brother Peter's side, taking the teardrop with him. Hereward watched him in dismay. He did not know how to ask for the medallion back, and without it he could never prove that it had existed at all. At least Brother Timothy did not know that he already possessed another of the teardrops.

At the same moment, Brother Padraig returned with the empty basket. Hereward made his farewells, eager to get back to the Crown and share what had happened with Gwyneth. One scarlet teardrop found at Chalcwelle, where Nathaniel de Bere had been murdered; another discovered in the infirmary at the abbey. What was the connection? Hereward wondered. Who had dropped it? Could it have been anything to do with Brother Timothy?

Hereward felt swamped by mystery, as if he was struggling in the marshes around the Tor, and he could see no way of reaching solid ground again.

Hereward's breath puffed out in a cloud as he guided Nathaniel de Bere's horse through the archway that led to the inn yard. That day had seen the first fall of winter snow, powdering the hills, though here in the village it had already been trampled to slush.

His spirits had been restored since his visit to

the abbey that morning. He had told Gwyneth about the second medallion as soon as he returned and they had discussed everything they had found out over and over without being able to decide what they should do. If they were to give the documents and the medallion to Finn Thorson or to Father Godfrey, they must do so soon. But that would be to admit defeat in finding the truth on their own. Gwyneth was still smarting over the way that Father Godfrey had warned them off. She was determined to carry on investigating, and Hereward knew just how stubborn she could be.

He did not often have the chance to ride such a magnificent animal as the dead pilgrim's horse—almost as good as Godfrey de Massard's black stallion—and had greatly enjoyed trotting the fine chestnut gelding along the quiet, snow-covered road as far as the bottom of the Tor and back again. Hereward could not imagine that they would be allowed to keep Master de Bere's horse at the Crown for long, but while it was here someone had to exercise it, and he had gladly offered.

The stable was warm with the breath of horses. Wat, one of the inn's servants, was clearing away a load of soiled straw. Greeting him, Hereward led the chestnut past two riding hacks and a mule belonging to visiting pilgrims, into a vacant stall at the far end.

'There,' he said, patting the glossy neck. 'I'll give you a good rub down, and Wat will bring you some hay. You'll like that, won't you?'

The horse whickered gently in reply. Hereward pulled off the saddle, hung it on a nail at the side of the stall, and removed the sweat-dampened saddle-cloth underneath to lay out in the yard to dry. As he folded it, he felt something stiff among the folds, and heard a crackling sound. Investigating more closely, he realized that one edge of the saddle-cloth had been folded back and stitched to make a pocket, with what felt like parchment concealed inside it.

Hereward glanced round; the stable was empty, except for Wat whistling tunelessly at the far end. He quickly picked at the thread on the saddle-cloth until he managed to unravel a few of the stitches and draw out what was inside.

His heart began to pound when he saw that he held two or three sheets of parchment, all of them closely covered with writing. Not daring to look at them there, he thrust them inside his tunic. Every muscle in his body urged him to dash out of the stable and find Gwyneth, but he made himself stay where he was and rub down the horse. When its coat shone like a polished chestnut, Hereward reminded Wat about feeding the gelding and made his escape.

The abbey bell was ringing for the afternoon service of nones as Hereward emerged into the yard to find Gwyneth scattering corn to the chickens that pecked around her feet.

'Finish that and come up to our room,' Hereward whispered. 'I've something you must see.'

Curiosity blazed in his sister's eyes. 'Can't you show me here?'

'No. Just come. And don't tell anyone.'

Hereward went inside and up to the little room under the eaves where he and Gwyneth slept. Although he was desperate to pull out the parchments and read them, he sat on his bed and forced himself to wait until he heard his sister's feet on the stairs.

'Well?' she said impatiently as she flung open the door. A few grains of corn clung to her skirt and she shook them onto the floor with a flick of her wrist.

'I was exercising Master de Bere's horse,' said Hereward, and he explained how he had found the pocket stitched in the saddle-cloth. 'These were inside,' he finished, drawing the parchments out of his tunic. 'Master de Bere must have hidden them, just as he hid the parchment in the water flask.'

'More letters?' Gwyneth flew across the room and sat beside Hereward on the bed, leaning over to see what he had found. 'It's almost as if Master de Bere is trying to tell us something from beyond the grave!'

Hereward scratched his chestnut hair. Sometimes he was impatient with his sister's flights of fancy, but for once he shared her feeling that the merchant's secrets were drawing them inexorably back into the mystery.

'Well, what do they say?' Gwyneth demanded. 'I hope they're not in Arabic this time!'

Hereward spread out the first of the parchments so they could read it together. It was nothing more than a scrap, addressed to Nathaniel de Bere; the handwriting was large and sprawling, unlike the neat hand in the letter from Father Herbert. It read: 'Very well. I will meet you in Glastonbury at the Crown, on the feast day of St Andrew. If I am not there, wait until I come.'

'The feast day of St Andrew? That was two days ago,' said Gwyneth. 'The day after Master de Bere arrived!' She frowned. 'But no one came to meet him.'

'Not at the inn—but they might have lain in wait for him somewhere else,' said Hereward. He felt a rapid fluttering in the pit of his stomach, and had to stop the hand that held the letter from shaking. 'Gwyneth, this could have been written by Master de Bere's murderer! They arranged to meet him here, but did not show themselves because they meant to commit a crime. If they knew he planned to visit Chalcwelle, they could have hidden there to ambush him.'

'But the letter's not signed.' Gwyneth sounded frustrated. Taking the scrap of parchment, she turned it over. A flash of scarlet caught Hereward's eye. At first he thought it was another teardrop, but then he realized that it was the fragment of a seal. The part that survived showed what looked like two arms of a cross, the ends branching into the petals of a lily.

'What a pity there's part of it missing!' said

Gwyneth. 'It might have told us who the murderer was.'

Hereward shook his head. 'I don't think a murderer would seal a letter with his own coat of arms.'

'He might not have meant to murder him when he wrote the letter,' Gwyneth pointed out. 'They could have had a quarrel, and he struck Master de Bere in a rage.' Setting the letter on one side, she added, 'Come on, let's look at the others!'

The other two sheets were bigger than the first, made of thicker, crackling parchment that had been folded to fit into the pocket in the saddle-cloth. They were covered with cramped handwriting; the first was headed in larger letters, and Hereward read out what it said. '"The Last Will and Testament of Nicholas de Bere".'

'Nicholas, not Nathaniel?' Gwyneth leant over to check for herself.

Hereward rapidly scanned the document. It seemed that Nicholas de Bere was an apothecary in London. His will left his business and a shop to his daughter and her husband, and a house, some money, and furnishings to his wife. There were small bequests of money to servants and a larger one to the Church. When Hereward came to the last item, his gaze fell on a familiar name.

'Here we are,' he said. '"*I leave to my beloved brother Nathaniel de Bere the sum of twenty pounds, in gratitude for the assistance he has agreed to give me.*" Nicholas de Bere must be our Master de Bere's brother.'

'What assistance does he mean, I wonder?' Gwyneth asked.

'It doesn't say,' said Hereward. 'Look at that,' he added. Underneath the signatures at the bottom of the will, a few words had been squeezed in, written in a different hand. 'My brother's body was recovered from the Thames this day: God have mercy on him,' he read aloud.

'So Nicholas drowned?' Gwyneth's eyes stretched wide with alarm. 'How many more people connected with this merchant have died?'

'It might have been an accident,' Hereward pointed out.

Gwyneth replied with a snort of disbelief. Instead of trying to argue, Hereward put the will down and began to examine the third and last sheet.

'This is another letter . . . and written by

Nicholas,' he said. "'To my dear brother Nathaniel . . .'"

'Here, let me,' Gwyneth said impatiently, seizing the letter as if she couldn't wait to make it give up its secrets. "'My fear grows daily",' she began, and her voice grew breathless as she continued, "'Would that I had never heard of Henry of Truro, or M, or this vile plot against King Richard.'"

She looked up; Hereward met her gaze with his heart plummeting. 'Henry of Truro is at the bottom of this!' he exclaimed hoarsely. 'Well, Father Godfrey will be satisfied to know that he's part of yet another crime. Go on.'

"'I regret the evil I have done in getting involved with this plot to murder an innocent man. My failing was that I fell into the sin of covetousness, for M's messenger offered me much gold. I confess that I sold him the poison knowing they would use it to murder King Richard's favourite priest, Father Aidan, and set another in his place to spy for Henry.'"

Gwyneth's hands clenched so tightly that Hereward was afraid she would crumple the letter. He reached out for it, but Gwyneth opened her fists again, taking a breath to calm herself.

'We have heard about this before,' she said. 'Don't you remember, when Master Green pretended his ale was poisoned?'

'The feast at Wells!' Hereward exclaimed. 'Uncle Owen said that Richard's priest was one of the guests. The poison must have been meant for him, and not Dean Alexander at all.'

Gwyneth read aloud from the letter again. '"Three others besides myself were embroiled in this wicked scheme. There was a woman in Wells who was charged with placing the poison in Father Aidan's favourite dish, and there was a priest from Smithfield who was to replace Father Aidan. Although we none of us met each other, we were all contacted in the first instance by the devil behind this dreadful plot, whom we knew only as M."'

'A priest from Smithfield!' Hereward dived for Gwyneth's bed at the opposite side of the room and rummaged under her mattress, where they had hidden the Arabic parchment and the letter from Father Herbert. 'Yes, that's right,' he added, waving the letter at Gwyneth. 'He signs it "Father Herbert of Smithfield". He must have been the priest who was going to replace Father Aidan.'

He felt even more baffled; one part of the

mystery was explained, but it was growing more complicated than he could have ever imagined. He returned to his bed and sat beside Gwyneth again. 'Is there any more?' he asked, nodding at Nicholas de Bere's letter.

Gwyneth began to read again. '"I cannot name any of these people, and yet I fear that M believes I know too much and might reveal the identity of my fellow sinners. Since the plot failed, I hear footfalls in the street behind me and tapping at my window. Brother Nathaniel, I beg of you, take care of my widow if the worst should happen, and see that my will is executed. Pray for me."'

Gwyneth sat back and put down the sheet. 'Nicholas told his brother Nathaniel about the plot,' she said, speaking half to herself. 'And after Nicholas died, Nathaniel managed to trace Father Herbert, and blackmailed him. Perhaps he found out about the woman from Wells, too, and this person called M that Nicholas was so afraid of. Perhaps he tried to blackmail them all!' She turned that intense gaze on Hereward. 'After his brother drowned? Was he *stupid*?'

'Stupid and greedy,' Hereward said bleakly. 'Listen,' he began. 'There were four people in the plot—'

73

'Nicholas de Bere, who provided the poison,' Gwyneth interrupted, counting them off on her fingers. 'Father Herbert, who was to take Father Aidan's place. This woman from Wells, who put the poison in the food . . . could she be working in the dean's kitchens, I wonder? And M, who was in charge of the whole thing. One of them must have killed Master de Bere to keep him quiet.'

'Well, it wasn't Nicholas,' said Hereward. 'He was already dead. And I don't think it can have been Father Herbert. If he wanted to kill Master de Bere he would do it in London, and there haven't been any visiting priests here in Glastonbury, as far as we know.'

'And he certainly didn't stay here,' Gwyneth agreed.

'There haven't been any women visiting from Wells, either,' Hereward went on; almost against his will he realized that he was set on fitting the pieces of the puzzle together. 'That just leaves M. And it was M that Nicholas de Bere was most afraid of.' He picked up the first letter again, the one appointing the Crown as a meeting-place. 'Perhaps this comes from M.'

Gwyneth brightened. 'At least we don't have

to suspect Brother Timothy any more,' she said. 'Or Ursus. Their names don't begin with M.'

'I'm not so sure.' Hereward felt uneasy. 'M might stand for monk—that could mean Brother Timothy. And I'm pretty sure that Ursus isn't his real name. It's no Christian name that I've ever heard of.'

Hereward could see that Gwyneth admitted the truth in what he was saying, even though she wanted to defend their friends. 'It can't have been . . .' she went on, and then jerked upright. 'Hereward, who else is there in Glastonbury whose name begins with M?' she demanded. 'Someone who comes from Wells?'

Hereward stared at her. 'Godfrey de Massard!'

Chapter Five

Hereward recalled the way the aristocratic young priest had looked coldly down at them as he warned them not to investigate the murder.

'That would explain why Father Godfrey wanted to take charge of the investigation,' said Gwyneth, echoing Hereward's own thoughts. 'And why he asked for all Master de Bere's things. If the merchant was trying to blackmail him as well as the other members of the plot, he would want to find out how much Master de Bere knew, and destroy anything that might reveal his crime.'

Hereward frowned. 'Yet it seems hard to believe that Father Godfrey could be involved in a plot that would help Henry of Truro,' he said, remembering the way the priest blamed any wrongdoing in the village on the traitor and his supporters.

'Father Godfrey only *says* that he's trying to

stop Henry of Truro,' Gwyneth retorted. 'We've never actually seen him catch a traitor, have we?'

'He was in the infirmary with Brother Padraig when I found the second medallion,' Hereward pointed out, half reluctant to add yet another item to weigh in the scale of Father Godfrey's guilt. 'He could have dropped it there.'

'Thank goodness we didn't pass those parchments on to him!' Gwyneth said. 'But what are we going to do now? Should we give all this to Master Thorson?'

'I don't know. He'll never believe that Father Godfrey could have anything to do with it without better evidence than the letter M. I think we should carry on with our seeking and expose him once and for all.'

'You're right.' Gwyneth's eyes flashed with determination as she gathered all the sheets of parchment together and stowed them away under her mattress. 'Somehow we've got to find a way of making Father Godfrey betray himself.'

That evening, Gwyneth sat on a stool in front of the fire in Marion le Fevre's bedchamber, tidying the embroidery threads in one of the shallow wicker baskets. The undemanding task kept Gwyneth's fingers busy while her mind was free to think about everything they had learnt. The embroideress had apparently recovered from her fear of murderers the previous day and was gossiping happily over her embroidery frame with Gwyneth's Aunt Anne, who came in every day to help her with her work.

There was the sound of rustling silk as Marion le Fevre got up from the frame and went to close the window shutters. 'No more for today,' she said. 'It grows late.'

'Owen will be coming home from the abbey soon,' said Anne Mason, rising to light the earthenware lamp. 'I must go and cook his supper.'

Before she had finished speaking, footsteps sounded in the passage outside and a knock came at the door. When Marion called, 'Enter!' it opened to reveal Owen Mason himself standing on the threshold.

'I thought I'd drop in and walk home with you,' he said to his wife, his face sombre. 'These days you never know who might be about.'

Marion le Fevre shuddered. 'Yes, dear Anne,' she agreed. 'You must not walk alone after dark.'

Uncle Owen walked over to the fire and stood

warming his hands, while Anne tidied away the embroidery patterns she had been tracing and fetched her cloak from where it lay across Marion's bed.

'Tomorrow you should leave early, or ask Wat or Hankin to see you home,' said Owen. 'You'll remember I have to go to Wells.'

Gwyneth jumped to her feet, scattering the skeins of silk that she had on her lap. 'Wells?'

'Yes.' Uncle Owen answered readily enough, though he looked puzzled at his niece's enthusiasm. 'I have business to see to, about the stone deliveries.'

'You could do me a great favour while you are there, Master Mason,' Marion put in.

'Of course, mistress.'

'I have great need of more silk and thread,' said the embroideress. 'I am sure Wasim Kharab will be at the market in Wells. Could you buy some for me?'

'It would be a pleasure, if you tell me what you need.'

'I will write it down,' said Marion, seating herself at her table and drawing quill, ink, and parchment towards her. 'Wasim knows the qualities I like, so be sure to tell him it's for me.'

Gwyneth collected the scattered silks and placed them neatly in the basket, wondering if there was any way that she and Hereward might go to Wells with their uncle. If Marion was right and Wasim Kharab was there, the Moorish merchant might be able to read the Arabic parchment for them. She couldn't help feeling that it was the glue that might bind all the pieces of this puzzle together.

She was considering how best to ask her uncle so that he was sure to say yes when there was another tap on the door and her mother appeared with a plate of honey cakes in her hand. Hereward followed her bearing a large, steaming jug.

'I thought you might like some refreshments,' Idony said, setting the plate on the table. 'And here is Hereward with hot water for you to wash before supper.'

'You look after me so well!' Marion exclaimed, glancing up with her quill poised in one hand. 'And Master Mason is good enough to do my errands for me on the morrow.'

'It's nothing,' said Owen, looking pleased at her praise. 'I'd be going to Wells anyway. Idony, is there anything I can get you while I'm there?'

'Wasim Kharab will be there,' Gwyneth put in, flashing a glance at Hereward.

Her brother turned away from setting down the water jug, his face suddenly interested.

'There certainly is,' Idony replied to Uncle Owen. 'Wasim Kharab has better spices than I can buy round here, and I could do with sewing thread, too, and perhaps—' She broke off, looking from Gwyneth to Hereward. 'Look at the pair of you! Panting like hunting dogs on the leash! Do you want to go to Wells with your uncle?'

'Yes, please!' Gwyneth begged, while Hereward nodded eagerly.

Idony hesitated, frowning. Gwyneth knew how nervous she had been since Father Godfrey had brought news of the murder to the Crown, and sent up an anguished prayer that her mother might not insist that they stayed at home. The chance of going to Wells so soon after the discovery of the parchment seemed almost miraculous, and she could hardly bear the thought that the opportunity might be lost.

'Please!' she repeated.

'Gwyneth wishes to see the bustle of the town,' Marion le Fevre remarked with an indulgent smile. 'So many pretty things for sale!'

Gwyneth's mother turned the frown on her, and then relaxed. 'Very well, you may,' she said. 'You will be safe enough with your uncle, and I can hardly keep you cooped up here all winter. I'll make a list for you of what I need from Wasim. Mind you don't pay too much, though.'

'We won't!' Gwyneth assured her.

She exchanged a triumphant glance with Hereward. Now they had a real chance of meeting Wasim Kharab again. He would read the parchment for them, and perhaps by this time tomorrow they would know why Nathaniel de Bere had been digging at Chalcwelle. If the parchment and the murder were connected, they might even be able to put a name to the poisoner and the mysterious M.

Chapter Six

Uncle Owen called at the Crown the next morning as the abbey bell rang for prime. To Gwyneth's relief, there had been no more snow during the night. She had been afraid that a heavy fall would have made the road impassable and prevented their journey to Wells. But as dawn broke, the sky was clear. Frost crackled under her feet as she and Hereward followed their uncle into the yard and climbed into the cart. Uncle Owen took up the reins, clicked his tongue at the mule, and they trundled out onto the road.

They were in time to see Godfrey de Massard striding along the street from the abbey, meeting Finn Thorson at the corner. The two men spoke urgently together; the breeze carried a few of the sheriff's words to Gwyneth's ears. '. . . Sim Short the basket-maker may have seen something.'

He and Father Godfrey set off in the direction of the marshes where Master Short lived.

Gwyneth wrapped herself into the folds of her cloak, drawing it tight against the biting cold. 'Have you got the money?' she asked Hereward. 'And the lists from mother and Mistress le Fevre? And . . .' She made a face, hoping that her brother would understand that she could not mention the parchment while Uncle Owen was listening.

'Yes,' Hereward said with a sigh. 'You know I have.' He pulled aside a fold of his tunic to show her the parchments tucked inside. 'You saw me put them there yourself.'

Gwyneth was about to reply when a voice hailed them from the side of the street and Ivo and Amabel Thorson dashed out of their house.

'We were coming to see you!' Amabel announced. 'Are you going somewhere?'

'Yes, to Wells,' Gwyneth replied.

Ivo snorted. 'Some people have all the luck!' Grinning to show he didn't mean to be unfriendly, he added, 'Anyway, it's your parents we need to speak to.'

'Father sent us,' Amabel continued, trotting alongside to keep up with the mule cart. 'He wants to find out where Master de Bere lived in London. He's going to send a message to his family. Then they can take his body to bury it.'

'Father can probably tell him,' said Hereward, and added, 'Does he know how Master de Bere died?'

'Hit over the head with a spade,' Ivo replied, beginning to pant from the brisk pace. 'He doesn't know who hit him, though. Not yet.'

He halted with Amabel beside him and both the twins waved as the mule cart drew away.

'Such wickedness,' Uncle Owen commented with a sigh. 'This used to be a peaceful place. Now I ask myself if there's any point in finishing the church, with such evil all around us. Still— one thing we can be sure of. Master de Bere brought his trouble with him.'

Gwyneth exchanged a glance with her brother. She wasn't at all sure any more that what her uncle said was true. When Master de Bere had come to Glastonbury, he had found trouble waiting for him.

The sun was high by the time the towers of Wells Cathedral appeared on the horizon. More travellers joined them on the road that led through the gates. Gwyneth pushed back her hood as the cart rolled into the city. There was so much to see: a bard striding along with his harp in a canvas case slung over one shoulder; a farm woman pushing a handcart loaded with turnips; a beggar in rags leaning on his staff with his hand held out for alms. Children chased a dog across the street and under the hooves of Uncle Owen's mule, nearly tripping a plump priest who was making his way towards the cathedral. The sounds of dogs barking, street traders crying their wares, and the ringing of the cathedral bells all made Gwyneth realize how different Wells was from Glastonbury.

The market-place lay just outside the walls that surrounded the cathedral. Gwyneth could not count the stalls, much less the people who crowded round them to bargain for the goods on offer. The press of people was so great that Uncle Owen could hardly steer a way through it.

Before long he drew the cart to a halt. 'I'll leave you here,' he said. 'The man I have to see lives down this street. Meet me by the gate over there, when the cathedral bell rings for sext. Then we'll have a bite to eat before we go home. Don't be late,' he added as Gwyneth and

86

Hereward scrambled down. 'Stay here in the market, mind, and speak only to traders.'

'We will,' Hereward promised as the cart rolled away.

'Now,' said Gwyneth. 'Where is Wasim Kharab?'

She looked around but there was no sign of the Moorish merchant's covered cart. Taking a deep breath, she plunged into the crowd with Hereward at her heels. 'Take care of the money,' she warned, glancing over her shoulder. 'There's bound to be cutpurses here.'

Wriggling her way along the lines of stalls, Gwyneth saw traders selling vegetables, honey, and gingerbread. Another stall had baskets of smooth brown eggs and live chickens hanging with their feet tied together from the wooden crossbar. Gwyneth began to feel uneasy; perhaps Marion had been wrong when she said Wasim would be in Wells that day.

As they forged on, the crowd seemed to get even thicker.

'This could take all day,' Hereward muttered.

Just then, Gwyneth heard a familiar sound: the thin wailing of a pipe, weaving its way through the crowds with a rhythm that seemed to tug her towards it. 'That's Wasim!' she exclaimed.

She made her way towards the music as quickly as she could. Soon she and Hereward came to the back of a tightly packed knot of people, standing round to look at something. Gwyneth stood on tiptoe, but failed to see over the heads and shoulders of the people in front of her. Hereward began to push his way through, and Gwyneth hurried to follow him before the crowd could close up again.

A reed mat had been placed on the ground in the middle of the spectators. On it a man sat cross-legged; he had a lean, hawkish face with glittering dark eyes and copper-coloured skin, and he was dressed in flowing white robes of fine linen. His fingers danced over the holes in the pipe to make the strange, reedy tune sing out. A sinuous black body rose from a basket in front of him, ending in a wide hood and a narrow head with a flickering forked tongue. Gwyneth felt a familiar jolt in her stomach as she recognized Wasim Kharab and his snake, Yasmin.

Behind him stood his covered cart, the backboard let down to display piles of brilliantly-coloured silks, copper bowls filled with spices, and delicately carved wooden boxes. A strong spicy scent filled the air. A squat figure, no taller than Gwyneth, appeared from round the front of the cart, hauling a sack.

Hereward grabbed Gwyneth's arm. 'It's Osbert Teller!' he hissed into her ear.

Gwyneth stared at the dwarf in amazement. Osbert Teller had once worked in Glastonbury as Rhys Freeman's assistant, but when the fake relics operation was exposed, he had fled the village. No one knew where he had gone, until now.

'We shouldn't be surprised,' Hereward went on quietly. 'Rhys Freeman was selling the relics to Wasim. It makes sense that Master Teller would go to him rather than suffer the stocks alongside his master.'

As he spoke, the piercing music came to an end. The snake gave one last bob of her head and sank back into the basket. Wasim clapped on the lid, and rose gracefully to bow to his audience. There was loud applause and several coins were tossed onto Wasim's mat. Gwyneth remembered the uncertain response that the merchant's show had received in Glastonbury, and reflected that the citizens of Wells must be more used to such exotic fare.

Meanwhile, Osbert Teller went over to Wasim.

'I've fed and watered the mules, master,' Gwyneth heard him say. 'I thought I'd go and get a sup of ale now.'

Wasim Kharab's eyes narrowed. 'My good Osbert, we have customers to attend to. There will be time later for all the ale you can drink.' Bowing once again to his audience, he announced, 'Here you may see all the treasures of the East. Come, see, touch, and we shall make a bargain that will be pleasing to all.'

As the townspeople began to move forward, Gwyneth and Hereward dodged round them and came to stand in front of the Moorish merchant, who was lifting the snake's basket into the back of his wagon.

'Good day, Master Kharab,' Hereward said boldly.

Gwyneth did not feel quite so brave. The last time they had met Wasim Kharab, they had been searching his cart, in the belief that he had stolen the cross that identified King Arthur's bones. Though he had sent them on their way with silken courtesy and gifts, she was not sure that he would be pleased to see them here in Wells.

But Wasim was smiling, his teeth flashing white against his saffron skin. 'Hereward and Gwyneth,

90

is it not? All the way from Glastonbury! Well met, my young friends.'

'They're no friends of mine,' Osbert Teller muttered. 'Young limbs of Satan!'

Wasim Kharab waved a hand at him dismissively. 'Go and serve our customers, Osbert,' he ordered. He turned and smiled at Gwyneth. 'Have you come to buy?' he asked. 'Or do you wish to search my cart again?'

Gwyneth felt herself going red. 'We need embroidery silks for Mistress le Fevre, and spices for mother,' she replied. 'But there's something we want to ask you, too.'

Hereward pulled out the lists from his tunic and handed them over to Wasim, who studied them carefully.

'Ah, the excellent Mistress le Fevre!' he said, raising his eyebrows. 'She is a lady who understands the finest materials. I must be sure not to disappoint her. Your mother too . . . Your inn should be famed throughout the land for her cooking.'

He rapidly collected the items on the lists and named a price that was well within what Idony and Marion had provided for.

'And now you must have your reward for doing

your errand so well,' he said while Hereward was counting out the money. 'What have we here?' One long-fingered hand swooped behind Gwyneth's ear and brought out a square of sweetmeat, studded with slivers of almond.

Though Gwyneth had seen his tricks before, the conjury still startled her; she laughed as he presented the sweetmeat to her, and bobbed a curtsy in thanks.

'And for your brother, too,' said Wasim, making another piece of the sweet stuff appear out of nowhere as Hereward handed him some coins.

'Thank you, Master Kharab,' said Hereward, taking the sweetmeat and biting into it appreciatively.

'And now . . .' Wasim went on, after a glance towards Osbert Teller, who was bargaining with a woman for a length of silk. 'What is this you wish to ask me?'

'It's this,' said Hereward, drawing out the parchment and handing it to the merchant. 'Someone told us it's written in Arabic. We wondered if you could read it for us.'

As Wasim began to read, Gwyneth saw his eyes widen and he froze until a pool of silence seemed to spread out from him into the busy market. When the merchant looked up again, his eyes were so sharp and glittering that they reminded Gwyneth of his snake.

'Where did you get this?' he demanded. Before either of them could reply, he flung up a hand for silence. 'No. Wait. These things should not be spoken of openly.' Turning to Osbert, he said, 'Stay here and guard the stall. And if I catch you listening to what we say, I will slice off your ear.'

The apprehensive look Osbert gave his master suggested to Gwyneth that he took the threat seriously.

Wasim held open the flap at the back of the cart so that Gwyneth and Hereward could scramble inside, avoiding the piles of merchandise on the backboard. When Gwyneth had last entered Wasim's cart, searching for the cross, she had been almost overwhelmed by the beauty and strangeness of the furnishings, so different from the plain wooden furniture and bare floorboards of the Crown. Even though she knew what to expect this time, she was still impressed.

The wooden framework that held up the

canvas cover of the cart was beautifully carved with leaves and flowers. The inside of the cover was draped with lengths of silk in brilliant colours, while the floor was spread with intricately patterned rugs. A silver lamp hung from one of the roof supports, although it was not lit at the moment and when Wasim Kharab let the flap fall back Gwyneth felt as if she was inside a shadowy cave, the air heavy with the smell of incense.

Wasim Kharab seated himself on a silken cushion and gestured to Gwyneth and Hereward to do the same. 'Where did you get this parchment?' he began.

'It belonged to a dead man.' Hereward explained how they had discovered the body of Nathaniel de Bere by Chalcwelle, and then found the parchment and the letter that went with it when the water flask had broken.

Wasim nodded gravely. 'It does not surprise me that a man has died for this.'

'What does the parchment say, Master Kharab?' Gwyneth asked, leaning forward. Her foot brushed a lidded basket, and she drew it back quickly when a faint hiss came from inside.

For a moment Wasim Kharab seemed reluctant to speak. 'It is a guide to the whereabouts of a great treasure,' he said at last.

'Then that's what Master de Bere was digging for up at Chalcwelle!' Hereward said slowly.

'And someone killed him to take the treasure for themselves,' Gwyneth concluded. Father Herbert's message had already told them the parchment spoke of the most precious thing in Christendom, but Wasim seemed to suggest that it was nothing less than a map.

Wasim tapped the parchment. 'This is old, my friends, very old. It was written by one of the companions of Joseph of Arimathea who came with him from the Holy Land to Britain.'

'And they came to Glastonbury.' Gwyneth's chest was suddenly so tight that she could hardly speak, and Hereward's eyes were round as the moon. 'The stories say they brought the Holy Grail—the cup of Christ.'

'Then is that . . . ?' Hereward could not go on.

Wasim Kharab nodded solemnly. 'Yes, my friends. The stories are true. The Holy Grail was buried in Glastonbury, near the spring you call Chalcwelle. This parchment gives directions how to find it.'

Gwyneth exchanged a glance with Hereward. 'We could go and look,' she whispered.

Her brother's eyes were shining, and Gwyneth knew that he was thinking the same as she was—that they could go to Chalcwelle, dig up the Holy Grail, and present it to the abbey. Pilgrims would flock from all over the world to see the most sacred relic of Jesus Christ.

Then Hereward shook his head. 'The murderer might have found it already. He might have dug it up after he killed Master de Bere.'

Gwyneth pressed a hand to her mouth, horrified by the thought of what a wicked man might do with the Holy Grail. If it fell into the hands of Henry of Truro, he could sell it for enough gold to pay for an entire army.

'I think not,' Wasim Kharab said. 'For now that I look more closely . . .' He bent over the parchment again, seeming to devour the words with his eyes. Then he looked up with a mixture of frustration and relief in his face. 'These instructions are not complete,' he said.

'What do you mean?' asked Hereward.

'The parchment reads, "A bird with but one wing will never fly. Go not to Chalcwelle unprepared, nor with greed and envy in your heart. Only two who are pure may achieve the Grail."'

Gwyneth thought for a moment. 'Does that mean there were *two* parchments?' she asked hesitantly.

'I think so,' said Wasim Kharab. 'I would guess that the man who made this wrote another also. The Grail will lie hidden until the two sets of directions are brought together again.'

'Then wherc is the other parchment?' said Hereward.

Wasim shrugged. 'The All-knowing God might tell you, but I cannot.'

'So why did Master de Bere bother digging at all?' said Gwyneth.

'The writing is in an ancient dialect,' Wasim explained. 'Even I have trouble in reading it. I would guess that Master de Bere's skill in my tongue was imperfect, and he thought that the document told him all that he needed to know. But the writer was subtle,' he added. 'This parchment tells the seeker to dig in the shadow of the rock from where Chalcwelle springs. But it does not say where the sun must be to cast the shadow in the right place.'

Hereward let out a grim laugh. 'He would have had to dig up half the hillside!'

'Perhaps he was prepared to do that, for such a treasure,' agreed Wasim.

'And he died for it,' Gwyneth said. She wondered if Father Herbert had known when he sent the parchment that it was almost worthless. Perhaps the priest was more cunning than his blackmailer anticipated after all.

'Master Kharab,' said Hereward, delving into his pouch and bringing out the scarlet teardrop, 'have you seen one of these before? It was sent to Master de Bere along with the parchment.'

'And it is pictured here,' said Wasim, touching the drawing of the medallion. 'No, I have never seen or heard tell of this before. I know nothing of what it might mean.'

Disappointed, Hereward returned the copper teardrop to his pouch. Wasim glanced once more at the parchment and then handed it back. 'Guard it well,' he said. 'Indeed, I would advise you to give it into the hands of someone better suited to guard it—your abbot, perhaps. Such treasures are dangerous, for they attract wicked men.'

As they thanked him and said their farewells, Gwyneth was chilled to think that Ursus had given them almost exactly the same warning. Perhaps their lives really were in danger. The lure of the Grail would tempt every man in Christendom. And yet there could be no turning back, for now they had to protect the holiest relic in the world from the hands of a murderer.

Chapter Seven

The sun had gone down, though its light still lingered in the sky when Uncle Owen's mule cart rolled down the main street and halted outside the Crown. Gwyneth and Hereward jumped down with the bundles they had bought in the market, and Gwyneth let out a huge sigh of relief as they thanked Uncle Owen and waved him off. She was fond of her uncle, but driving back from Wells with him had been torture when all she wanted to do was discuss what Wasim had told them.

'We'll have to help mother with supper,' she said as the cart trundled off into the twilight. 'And *then* maybe we can decide what to do next.'

They were about to turn into the inn yard when Gwyneth spotted a black-clad figure walking along the other side of the street towards the abbey. It was Brother Timothy. When he saw them he raised a hand in greeting and hurried across the street to join them.

'I'm sorry about yesterday, Hereward,' he began. 'I was sharp with you, in the infirmary.'

'It was nothing,' said Hereward, looking wary and clutching the parchment closer to him under the folds of his tunic.

'No, I should not have spoken so. It is just that I am grievously worried about Brother Peter.' A shadow fell across the young monk's bony features, and Gwyneth felt—as she had felt so often just lately—that he was no longer the cheerful, uncomplicated friend they had known for so long. 'His cough troubles him,' Brother Timothy went on, 'and in such bitter weather he . . . he might not live for much longer.'

'Oh, no!' Gwyneth said. 'Brother Padraig must know what to do for him.'

Brother Timothy forced a smile. 'Perhaps. But Brother Peter is very old, and something tells me God is calling him. What worries me most . . .' He hesitated as if he was not sure whether to go on. 'There is something troubling him,' he said at last. 'I know he has not made his confession to Father Abbot and I fear that his spirit cannot be at peace until he does.'

Gwyneth hardly knew what to say, and Brother Timothy did not wait for a reply. Shaking his head briskly, he said, 'Well, he is in God's hands,' and strode on towards the abbey. She watched him until he vanished through the gateway. 'Do you really think he might be M?' she whispered. 'Could he have arranged the whole poisoning plot?'

'I don't know,' Hereward admitted. 'But there's more than he told us troubling him, I'm sure. Brother Peter isn't the only person in the abbey with something on his mind.'

Agreeing with him, Gwyneth was about to lead the way into the yard when she heard the sound of horses' hooves approaching. In the lead was a lady riding a pretty white palfrey, with several servants following, and a mule cart stacked with bundles bringing up the rear.

'Visitors!' Hereward exclaimed. 'Do you think they're coming here?'

Before Gwyneth could reply, the lady swept past and guided her mount under the archway that led to the inn yard, followed by her escort and the cart. Gwyneth and Hereward quickly followed to find a scene of confusion, with the lady herself still mounted while her servants shouted for service and chickens fled squawking from the trampling feet of the horses. Wat appeared from the stables at a run and one of the servants, who were all wearing smart outfits of dark green wool, stepped forward to speak urgently to him.

'We'll tell father!' Hereward called to Wat.

He and Gwyneth hurried inside. There was no sign of Geoffrey Mason in the taproom or the kitchen; they found him at last with their mother in the counting room at the back of the inn, with parchments and piles of coins spread out on the table between them.

'I doubt we'll see any payment of Nathaniel de Bere's debt,' Geoffrey was saying, tossing a piece of parchment onto the table. 'And what about that horse? It costs more to feed than we do.'

He looked up as Gwyneth and Hereward burst through the door. 'There you are at last! Did you have a good journey?'

'Was Wasim Kharab there?' Idony Mason added.

'Yes, and we got everything you wanted.' Gwyneth made a space on the table to put her bundles down. 'That's Mistress le Fevre's thread, and here are your spices, and—'

'And there's a party of new guests out in the

yard,' Hereward interrupted. 'A lady and her servants. She looks rich indeed—she has a splendid horse!'

'Well, that's good news.' Geoffrey Mason got to his feet, a few of the parchments he had been sorting still in his hand.

'What does a fine lady want here?' Idony asked fretfully. 'Hasn't she heard about the murder?'

She paused at the sound of rapid footsteps in the passage outside; a moment later the lady herself swept into the room. She was a tall woman about Idony's age, with pale gold hair gathered up into a fashionable head-dress. Her gown was crimson velvet, richly embroidered at the neck and wrists; if she dressed like that for travelling, Gwyneth thought, what must her best gowns be like? Over the crimson dress she wore a fur-lined cloak, and pearls gleamed in her ears and on her fingers.

'You are the innkeeper?' the visitor asked Geoffrey.

Geoffrey bowed respectfully. 'Yes, my lady.'

'Then perhaps you can sort out this foolish error. I am Lady Isabelle Carfax. Your servant has just dared to show me to an inferior bedchamber—little better than a closet! He tells me you have better, but refuses to take me there.'

Gwyneth noticed that Hankin was hovering red-faced in the passage. He must have shown her to the chamber which Nathaniel de Bere had occupied—the only one in the inn which was suitable for a wealthy guest, except for the room where Marion le Fevre was staying.

'I'm sorry, my lady.' Geoffrey Mason gave another bow. 'There is indeed one better room, but it is already occupied.'

'Then the occupant will have to move! Take me there at once. And find somewhere for my servants to stay.'

Geoffrey exchanged a glance with his wife, and said, 'Very well, my lady. And perhaps you would care for a cup of wine after your journey? Hankin, go and see to Lady Isabelle's escort.'

Evidently relieved, the servant scurried away. Gwyneth beckoned to Hereward and darted up the stairs ahead of her father and the new guest, in the hope of giving Marion le Fevre a little warning that her privacy was about to be invaded. Tapping on Marion's door, she went in to discover the embroideress tidying away the day's work.

She looked up and gave Gwyneth her brilliant smile. 'My dear! Did you enjoy your day?'

'Yes, it was wonderful, and here are all your things.' Gwyneth set the list and the package of embroidery silks down on the table. 'But, mistress, there's a—'

Footsteps were already sounding outside, and before Gwyneth had the chance to explain, a tap came on the door. Her father opened it and gestured to Lady Isabelle Carfax, who stalked into the room; clearly she had refused the offer of wine made just now. She halted inside the doorway and gazed around.

'This is the best you have, you say? Well, it is not what I am used to, but I suppose it will have to do.'

Marion le Fevre drew herself up. 'Your pardon, mistress?'

'I am Lady Isabelle Carfax. You will address me as "my lady", and you will remove yourself and your belongings from this chamber immediately. I'm sure that the innkeeper will be able to find you a room elsewhere quite suitable for your station.'

Marion raised a hand in confusion. 'Master Mason?'

'I'm sorry, mistress.' Geoffrey Mason was bright red with discomfort, nervously rustling the bills that he still held in his hands. 'Would it be too inconvenient for you to change rooms? I'm sure it would only be for a few days.'

'But the light is good here,' Marion protested, a glimmer of steel in her voice like a half-sheathed sword. 'I need it for my work.'

'Your *work*?' Lady Isabelle enquired, with a lift of her fine eyebrows. 'Ah, your stitchery, I see.' She swept across the room to stand in front of Marion's embroidery frame, which displayed a length of silk superbly embroidered with lilies.

'Mistress le Fevre is an embroideress,' said Gwyneth. Her voice came out louder than she meant, as she tried to control the anger which was beginning to boil inside her. 'She's doing the most beautiful work for the abbey. This is an altar cloth for the Lady Chapel, no less.'

Lady Isabelle didn't seem to hear. After examining the silk for a moment she turned away and announced, 'I am here to visit Abbot Henry. I intend to make a large donation to the abbey in memory of my late husband. No doubt it will enable the abbot to go on employing you for a little longer,' she added.

Marion le Fevre tightened her lips. 'No doubt, my lady,' she said in a voice like ice.

'Then you won't mind moving?' Geoffrey Mason took Marion's response as agreement, though Gwyneth could see he was embarrassed. Dropping the parchments on the table, he added, 'I'll help you carry your things, of course.'

'So will we,' said Hereward. He picked up one of the bundles that contained Marion le Fevre's fabrics and carried it out, raising his eyebrows at Gwyneth as he passed her.

Geoffrey Mason lifted the embroidery frame. 'We'll take great care of everything,' he promised.

Mistress le Fevre gave him a tiny nod. Gwyneth saw that she had gone quite white, and she was almost afraid that the sensitive woman might faint, until she realized that her eyes were glittering with rage. A sharp snap made Gwyneth jump; Marion had been gripping one of her ivory bobbins so tightly that it had broken.

Lady Isabelle seated herself by the table and surveyed the room with satisfaction. 'I shall take my meals here,' she informed Geoffrey as he returned for another load. 'My own cook will prepare them.'

Gwyneth had to press her lips together to stop herself from blurting out something rude. As if her mother's cooking wasn't good enough! Hot with anger, she snatched up one of the baskets of silk and was just leaving when she remembered the new threads left on the table.

Turning back to collect them, she saw that Lady Isabelle's gaze had fallen on the parchments Geoffrey Mason had abandoned there. She had frozen into stillness, one hand hovering above the table. The haughty satisfaction had drained away from her expression, leaving a look of pure horror in her eyes.

Gwyneth stared. What could there be on the table that should make Lady Isabelle Carfax look so afraid?

Chapter Eight

'You may all go now,' Lady Isabelle said shakily. She had brought her fear under control in the time it had taken to remove the rest of Marion le Fevre's possessions from the bedchamber, though Gwyneth thought she was finding it hard to keep her voice steady. 'Please send my cook up to take my order for supper.'

'Yes, my lady.' Geoffrey Mason bowed and retreated, taking Gwyneth and Hereward with him. As soon as the door had closed behind them he let out a long sigh. 'Sweet saints, what a tyrant!' he muttered. 'I'd willingly send her packing, but we need her gold, more's the pity.'

'I'm going to help Mistress le Fevre settle in,' said Gwyneth.

'Yes, do that,' her father agreed, 'but find your mother first and ask her for fresh bed linen for Lady Isabelle. Hereward, you can go to the stable,' he added. 'See that Lady Isabelle's horse is being cared for.'

Hereward clattered off down the stairs. Gwyneth followed more slowly to fetch the bed linen. When she went back into the bedchamber with the clean sheets, Lady Isabelle had taken off her cloak and was studying her face in a small silver mirror.

'Leave the linen there, girl,' she ordered. 'My maid will make up the bed. And fetch me hot water.'

Gwyneth curtsied and was leaving when Lady Isabelle stopped her. 'Are there any letters awaiting me here?'

'I don't think so, my lady,' Gwyneth replied. 'I'll ask my father, and if there are any I'll bring them up.'

But when she found Geoffrey Mason and asked him, there were no messages at all for Lady Isabelle Carfax.

By the time Gwyneth had passed on the order to Lady Isabelle's maid and helped Marion to put away her things and organize her work for the next day, the hour of supper was approaching. When she went into the kitchen to help her mother, she found Hereward by the fire, turning

111

the spit where three fat geese were roasting, while Idony pulled loaves out of the bread oven.

A stranger was standing beside the table. He was tall and thin, with a balding head and small, dark-brown eyes.

'This is Master Bernard,' Idony said in a clipped voice that told Gwyneth that her mother was annoyed. 'He is Lady Isabelle's cook. Please be ready to help him if he needs.'

'Yes, mother,' said Gwyneth. 'Good evening, Master Bernard.'

Master Bernard was slicing up what looked like the finest venison. 'Fetch me a pot, girl,' he ordered without looking up.

Gwyneth shot a glance at Idony, who rolled her eyes in exasperation and began to pile the loaves into baskets. At least, Gwyneth thought, her anger towards the arrogant cook had distracted her mother from her fear of murderers. Reminding herself of the need to be polite to guests and their servants, she fetched the pot and handed it to Master Bernard, who poked his long nose into it and thrust it back at her.

'Scrub it.'

Gwyneth needed all her self-control to bob a curtsy and take the perfectly clean pot out to the scullery to wash it again. When she brought it back, Master Bernard gave it a close inspection and ungraciously decided that it would do. He placed the venison in it and began to chop onions, pausing for a moment to prod a veal pie of Idony's that was cooling on the table. 'What's that?' he asked, twitching his nose. 'Veal? A poor thing. I cooked far better at the last feast I prepared.'

Gwyneth had gone to the fire to stir the pot of bean soup. 'Horrible man!' she whispered to Hereward, who was turning the spit vigorously to work off his anger. 'Mother's pies are the best in all England!'

Tasting the soup, she decided it needed more parsley, and fetched some from a heap of the chopped herb on the table close to where Master Bernard was working. As she sprinkled it into the pot of soup, he exclaimed, 'God's bones, girl! Have you just stolen my parsley?'

'Oh, I'm so sorry, Master Bernard,' Gwyneth said, hearing a muffled chuckle from Hereward behind her. 'I didn't realize it was yours.'

The cook snorted. 'This isn't what I'm used to,' he said, apparently speaking to Idony, though she carried on with her tasks without paying much attention to him. 'Not in Lady Isabelle's kitchen, nor yet when I used to work for Dean Alexander at Wells.'

Out of the corner of her eye, Gwyneth saw that Hereward had paused from turning the spit. 'Dean Alexander?' he echoed. 'Did you really work for him?'

'I did,' Master Bernard replied smugly. 'He kept a good table. My skill was much appreciated.'

'Hereward!' Idony exclaimed as she whisked past with a basket of bread in her hands. 'You're letting the geese burn.'

Hereward jumped and began turning the spit again, flashing a look at Gwyneth as he did so. Gwyneth's chest felt tight. If Master Bernard had worked in Dean Alexander's kitchens, he might know something about the poisoning plot which linked all the shadowy figures behind Master de Bere's letters.

'You must have cooked for some very important people,' she prompted.

'The highest in the land,' said Master Bernard. He gave Gwyneth a suspicious look. 'Get to your tasks, girl. There's no time for gossiping.'

Finishing off his venison dish with a sprinkling of salt, he took the pot to the fire and hung it above the flames.

'Have you worked for Lady Isabelle long?' asked Hereward.

'A month or so.' Master Bernard wiped his hands on his apron and went over to one of the remaining trays of loaves, turning them over as if he was looking for one fit to serve to his mistress.

'She sounds as if she would be hard to please,' Hereward ventured.

'She is that,' Master Bernard agreed. 'You wouldn't believe some of the stories I could tell! Why, we should have been here three days ago but that white horse of hers went lame, and was there another good enough? There was not, so we had to wait until he was fit to ride again.'

For a moment he had relaxed as if he was glad of the chance to have a good grumble, but almost at once he turned his back on Hereward and his voice was sharp again as he spoke to Gwyneth. 'Find me some butter, girl—good and fresh, mind. And wine, if there's anything here fit for my lady to drink.'

Gwyneth curtsied and went to do his bidding. She felt disappointed that she had not persuaded Master Bernard to say more. He must know more than the gossip of the village about the poisoning at Wells, but he was such an unfriendly man that the information would stay locked in his head. Gwyneth could not see any way to get it out.

More snow fell overnight, and the air next morning was colder than ever. Gwyneth was grateful for the warmth of the kitchen as she helped her mother to knead the bread, and reluctant to leave when her father called to her from the inn yard.

'I want you and Hereward to escort Lady Isabelle to the abbey,' he explained.

Hereward was already waiting in the yard, stamping his feet to keep them warm, and by the time Gwyneth fetched her cloak Lady Isabelle had appeared, splendidly dressed in a blue velvet gown embroidered with pearls. She held up the hem to keep it clear of the trampled snow, and picked her way across the yard in her fine leather shoes.

She did not deign to reply to Gwyneth and Hereward when they wished her good morrow, but allowed them to lead the way out of the yard and along the street towards the abbey. The pale sun cast blue shadows over the surface of the snow. The market-place was deserted, the stalls covered in a white blanket, and most windows were shuttered against the cold. The only other person on the street was the firewood seller, struggling to push his cart through the drifts outside the abbey gate.

Geoffrey Mason had judged the time well, for the monks were just leaving the Lady Chapel as Gwyneth and Hereward arrived with their guest in the abbey precinct. One of the first to appear was Godfrey de Massard. When he saw Lady Isabelle he halted with a look of curiosity on his face, and then came over to her.

'Good morrow, Lady Isabelle,' he said, bowing stiffly. His face was lined by weariness, and Gwyneth wondered grimly what was keeping him awake at night. 'I hardly expected to see you here.'

'Nor I you, Father Godfrey,' Lady Isabelle replied. 'I am surprised that your duties do not keep you in Wells.'

'At present my duties keep me here,' the priest explained. 'I have been charged with investigating the murder of a man named Nathaniel de Bere.'

Gwyneth watched Lady Isabelle's face grow

tense as she spoke to Father Godfrey; clearly there was no love lost between the two of them. Alarm flared into the woman's eyes when he told her about the murder, and she let out a gasp of terror. 'Murder?' she whispered, pressing one trembling hand to her throat.

'His head was crushed by an iron spade.' It seemed Father Godfrey felt no need to soften the brutal details of Master de Bere's death for Lady Isabelle. 'But I have no doubt that I shall soon discover the culprit. I have all Master de Bere's possessions to examine, and I have written to London for news of his dealings there.'

'Indeed?' Lady Isabelle made an effort to control herself. 'Then I am sure you will succeed, Father Godfrey, and the sooner the better. I had no idea I was coming into a nest of murderers.'

'One murderer only, I trust,' said Father Godfrey. 'And he may already be far from here, as Master de Bere most certainly brought the reason for his death with him.'

Gwyneth gave her brother a quick glance; could Godfrey de Massard speak with such easy inno-cence if he was M himself, and de Bere's murderer as well as the person behind the poisoning at Wells? Either he was a better actor than any she had seen in the yearly mumming plays, or he was not guilty of Nathaniel de Bere's murder after all.

'And now perhaps you could conduct me to Abbot Henry,' Lady Isabelle went on. 'I must speak with him regarding a donation to the abbey.'

'Then this is the man you need.' Father Godfrey beckoned to Brother Barnabas, the abbey steward. 'He will be able to tell you where your money will be best spent.'

'But I wish to speak to the abbot.' Lady Isabelle's voice was steely. 'It will be a very *large* donation.'

'My lady.' Smiling, Brother Barnabas bowed to her. 'Abbot Henry is at prayer, but I am the abbey steward, and I will be delighted to show you round. In a short while I'm sure that the abbot will be free to discuss the matter with you.'

Lady Isabelle was still clearly displeased, but she bowed her head. She dismissed Gwyneth and Hereward with a wave of the hand as she followed Brother Barnabas into the Lady Chapel.

Gwyneth dropped a curtsy to Father Godfrey, and she and Hereward turned to go. Glancing back over her shoulder, she saw that the priest was gazing after the visitor with a puzzled frown on his face. It was hardly surprising that he had known Lady Isabelle in Wells if she had had dealings with the cathedral, but there seemed more to their relationship than mere social acquaintance. Gwyneth would have given a great deal to know exactly what he was thinking.

Balancing a tray in one hand, Gwyneth tapped on the door of Lady Isabelle's bedchamber and let herself in. The lady had returned from the abbey not long before, and her cook had prepared a dish of coddled eggs and cream for her midday meal.

To Gwyneth's surprise, Marion le Fevre was in the room with Lady Isabelle, who was seated at the table with a quill in her hand. The embroideress seemed to be showing her some designs.

'Of course, my lady,' she was saying as Gwyneth entered, 'if you wish to pay for a new set of vestments I could certainly include your coat of arms in the pattern.' She sounded very respectful; her anger at the change of rooms seemed to have vanished like dew.

'I will think on it,' Lady Isabelle replied,

glancing up at Gwyneth. 'Put your tray down here, girl,' she ordered, 'and then wait. I have an errand for you.'

She added a few words to the letter she was writing, signed her name and wafted the sheet of parchment in the air to dry the ink. Gwyneth peered sideways at it as she set down the tray, but was unable to read anything but the flamboyant signature.

'I wish you to take this to the abbey,' Lady Isabelle went on, folding the sheet and holding a stick of wax to the lamp flame to soften it. 'Deliver it into the hand of Father Godfrey de Massard.'

Gwyneth started with surprise, and hoped Lady Isabelle had not noticed. Why should their guest be writing to Father Godfrey? They had spoken together less than two hours ago.

To her relief, Lady Isabelle had seen nothing. She dropped hot wax on the folded letter, and pressed her seal ring firmly down on it. Handing it to Gwyneth, she said, 'Here you are. Take it at once, and be sure not to drop it.'

Gwyneth caught a sympathetic glance from Marion le Fevre as she slipped out of the room and went to fetch her cloak.

Idony Mason clicked her tongue when Gwyneth explained Lady Isabelle's order. 'Has she not enough servants of her own to run around after her? Very well, Gwyneth, you may go, but hurry back. I need you to help pluck the chickens for tonight's supper.'

'Yes, mother,' said Gwyneth, escaping into the inn yard.

'Take Hereward with you!' her mother called after her. 'And speak to no strangers on the way!'

In the yard, Gwyneth caught sight of Hereward coming out of the stables and beckoned him over. 'Look at this—Lady Isabelle is writing to Father Godfrey. What do you think it means?'

Hereward took the letter and glanced at it, and then froze, staring at the seal. 'Gwyneth, have you seen this?'

'What's the matter?'

'Don't you recognize it?' He thrust the letter under her nose so that she could clearly see the coat of arms on the seal: a cross with each of the arms spreading out into the petals of a lily.

Gwyneth gasped. 'But that's—'

'Come on!' Not waiting to see if she was following, Hereward charged back into the inn and up the stairs to their bedroom. When

Gwyneth arrived, puffing, he was already burrowing under her mattress, and reappeared with Nathaniel de Bere's parchments clutched in one hand.

'Look!' he said.

He thrust out the scrap of parchment which announced the appointment to meet Master de Bere at the Crown. The scrap of seal exactly matched the one on Isabelle Carfax's letter.

'You know what that means, don't you?' Hereward's hazel eyes were huge. 'Lady Isabelle Carfax is one of the poisoners!'

Chapter Nine

'Nathaniel de Bere must have been blackmailing her, just as he blackmailed Father Herbert,' Gwyneth panted as she and Hereward hurried along the street towards the abbey. 'Nicholas's letter mentioned a woman from Wells, and that's where Lady Isabelle comes from. The priest sent Nathaniel the document about the Holy Grail in payment for keeping quiet about the plot. I wonder what Lady Isabelle was going to give him?'

'I don't know,' said Hereward. 'Her cook used to work for Dean Alexander. He said he left about two months ago, close to the time of Dean Alexander's feast. He must have been the one who put the poison in the dish of venison.' He halted, frowning. 'He took a big risk. He could have been hanged.'

'I expect he'd arranged to escape,' said Gwyneth, urging her brother on down the snow-covered street. 'And Lady Isabelle would have paid him well.'

'Nathaniel de Bere discovered that she was involved after his brother died and left all those letters,' Hereward went on. 'He began to blackmail her and arranged to meet her at the Crown. But she was delayed because her horse went lame, and de Bere was murdered before he could keep their appointment.'

'It's all making sense now,' Gwyneth agreed. 'Lady Isabelle asked if there were any messages when she first arrived because she was expecting to see Nathaniel de Bere. Remember how frightened she seemed when Father Godfrey mentioned he had been murdered?'

Hereward looked puzzled. 'I would have thought she would feel relieved, to hear that her blackmailer was dead.'

'She was afraid before, too,' Gwyneth went on, remembering. 'When she first went into Mistress le Fevre's bedchamber.'

'I can guess why,' Hereward told her. 'Father left some parchments on the table, and one of them was a bill with de Bere's signature on it. It must have been quite alarming, to think she was so close to her blackmailer, who knew the truth of her part in the poisoning.'

Gwyneth whirled round to face her brother under the abbey gateway. 'You know what this means, don't you?' She flourished Lady Isabelle's letter at him. 'She must have written to Father Godfrey because he is M! They were in the poisoning plot together!'

'I don't see how the letter proves that,' Hereward said doubtfully.

'Because Lady Isabelle knows that Father Godfrey has all Master de Bere's things,' Gwyneth explained. 'She'll want to make sure that her letter to Master de Bere is destroyed, along with anything else that could identify her. She will be as keen as Father Godfrey to ensure that the poisoners are never revealed.'

Hereward nodded in agreement. 'I have to say,' he added, 'if she knows what happened to Nicholas and Nathaniel de Bere, she's taking a great risk by writing to M. It sounded as though that was the person Nicholas was afraid of most.'

'You're right,' said Gwyneth. 'I certainly wouldn't like to be mixed up with someone like M.'

A chill was creeping over her and she realized they had been standing for too long in the snow.

She beckoned to Hereward, and the two of them went into the abbey grounds.

The snow-covered precinct was deserted. The service of sext would be over by now, and the monks would be at their meditation. The icy weather had brought work to a halt and there was no sound of hammering coming from the new church.

'I wonder where Father Godfrey is,' Gwyneth said.

Before Hereward could reply, a black-robed figure emerged from the abbey kitchens and began the trek across the snow towards the infirmary. Hereward sprinted off to meet him while Gwyneth, hampered by her skirt, followed more slowly. As she drew closer, she saw that the monk was Brother Timothy, and came up in time to hear him say, 'No, Hereward, I have not seen Father Godfrey since sext. You might try his room in the guest lodgings.'

'Thank you,' said Hereward.

'How is Brother Peter?' Gwyneth asked, with a pang of guilt that they had ever suspected Brother Timothy of being M. It was a relief to be able to trust their friend again, now that they were sure Father Godfrey was behind the poisoning.

'Brother Peter is still very ill,' Brother Timothy replied, a troubled look creeping over his face. 'In both his body and mind. It grieves us all deeply.' He showed them a covered cup which he held carefully in both hands and added, 'Brother Milo has brewed him a hot posset. I must take it to him quickly before it gets cold.'

'Tell him we hope he's better soon,' Hereward said as Brother Timothy moved away.

The young monk glanced back over one shoulder. 'Pray for him,' he begged.

Gwyneth and Hereward watched his solitary progress across the snow before turning back towards the guest lodgings. Close to the door, Gwyneth paused; the twisted branches of the Holy Thorn tree that grew in the abbey grounds, one of those descended from Joseph of Arimathea's staff, had begun to put out their first fragile flowers, white as snowflakes clinging to the grey-green bark. Gwyneth remembered the story of the saint who had planted the first Thorn and brought the Holy Grail to Britain; could the flowers be a sign of hope that she and Hereward would bring the truth to light? Sighing, she turned away. She could not be sure, and there was no point in telling the ever-practical Hereward about her imaginings.

When they knocked at Father Godfrey's door, a curt voice said, 'Enter.'

Hereward pushed open the door to reveal Father Godfrey seated beside a bright fire, with Nathaniel de Bere's belongings spread out around him. He half rose as the door opened but sank back in his chair when he saw who it was.

'What do you want?' he demanded.

Gwyneth ventured into the room, her heart thudding at the thought of being in the presence of a man who almost certainly had murdered more than once. She noticed that Hereward stayed beside the open door, guarding their retreat.

Curtsying, she held out the letter. 'Lady Isabelle Carfax sent you this, sir.'

Father Godfrey looked faintly surprised. Taking the letter he broke the seal and spread out the sheet. 'Wait for a moment,' he said. 'There may be a reply.'

Once again Gwyneth tried to see what was written in the letter, but she was looking at it upside down, and Lady Isabelle's handwriting was difficult to read. Whatever it was, it held

129

Father Godfrey's attention, for his look of surprise deepened and he read it through two or three times. He frowned thoughtfully, and when he looked up his eyes were deep and dark.

'I need not write an answer,' he said to Gwyneth. 'Tell the lady I will do as she asks.' He crumpled the letter, destroying any chance Gwyneth had of reading it, and tossed it into the fire.

'I wonder what Lady Isabelle wants him to do,' Hereward said as they plodded back through the snow.

'Nothing good.' A shiver ran through Gwyneth that had nothing to do with the cold weather. 'Did you see that brooding look? As if he was plotting something? And he burnt the letter,' she added. 'I'm sure he was destroying evidence against him!'

As they approached the abbey gateway, Gwyneth halted. 'Let's go to the chapel,' she suggested. 'I want to say a prayer for Brother Peter.'

But when she stood in front of the altar, she found that more thoughts were crowding through her mind. She murmured a few words asking for the old monk's quick recovery, but there were so many other troubles she hardly knew what to pray for.

The letter from Lady Isabelle and Father Godfrey's reaction to it had made her fairly sure that he was the murderer, the traitorous M who murdered Nathaniel de Bere because he was blackmailing all the people involved in the poisoning plot. The only person they might tell was Finn Thorson, but he would never believe them with so little evidence. They could hardly add to Brother Timothy's troubles when he was sick with worry about Brother Peter. Ursus, too, whom they had trusted almost from the beginning, had roused their suspicions; even if he was not the murderer, he was hiding something from them.

Gwyneth rested her hand on the ancient oaken coffin which held the bones of King Arthur and Queen Guinevere. She imagined she could feel warmth soaking into her from those precious relics, which lay here now thanks to her and Hereward's efforts to find them several months ago.

I wish you were here now, King Arthur, she thought silently. *You would show us what we ought to do.*

* * *

By now, the Crown was packed with visitors; the bitter weather had not deterred the usual pilgrims, and besides them there was an influx of travellers eager to see the place where a murder had been committed. The rush of business kept Gwyneth and Hereward busy all day and into the following morning.

'I can't understand it,' remarked Idony Mason, pausing to push back a strand of hair as she hurried into the taproom with a basket of loaves. 'Are they mad? Why do people want to gawp at the place where a man was murdered, when they could stay safe in their own homes?'

'I'm tired of telling them the way to Chalcwelle,' Geoffrey Mason agreed. 'It seems strange to come all this way in the snow. But who am I to complain?'

After the mid-day meal, Gwyneth and Hereward were sitting on stools in front of a roaring fire in the kitchen. Gwyneth was mending a hole in her stocking, while Hereward repaired a piece of harness. Smoke billowed out from the fire, setting Gwyneth coughing, as her father opened the door from the inn yard and came inside, stamping snow off his boots.

'How would you two like to go and gather

firewood?' he asked. 'We're running low.'

'Lady Isabelle has sent down three times for logs since this morning,' Idony put in, looking up from the table where she was grinding spices in a mortar. 'She's enough up there now to roast a dozen oxen,' she complained, crossly stabbing a clove with the pestle. 'She went out as soon as she had eaten her meal, so her room is being heated for nothing.'

'We'll go out now.' Gwyneth jumped up, pleased with any excuse to leave her mending, which made her eyes ache and left her fingers covered with needle pricks, as if she'd been juggling hedgepigs.

Hereward looked more reluctant to leave the fire, but he went out to the stables to fetch their mule, and led it into the yard with panniers slung over its back to carry the wood. With a small axe in his free hand he led the mule into the street, while Gwyneth kept pace on the other side.

'Let's not go too close to the river,' she said. 'I'm not sure I want to meet Ursus today.' Guilt stabbed at her, sharp as a knife; she felt as if she was betraying their friend by her certainty that he was keeping something back from them.

'Better not,' Hereward replied, as if he understood.

Instead of taking the direct route to the river, they turned up Tor Lane and headed into the woods on the lower slopes of the Tor, not far from Chalcwelle. Snow blanketed the ground under the trees and lay heavy on the branches, the white covering broken here and there by coils of dark green holly and ivy. A grey sky lowered overhead, heavy with more snow to come. Everything was still; even the sound of their footsteps was muffled and the air tingled with cold.

Hereward cleared a patch of snow so that the mule could forage for the sparse winter grass before he and Gwyneth set to work. Warmed through by the effort of dragging the branches that Hereward had cut down, Gwyneth was beginning to enjoy herself when she heard a noise some distance away. She halted with one end of the branch still clutched in her hands.

Hereward paused with his axe raised. 'What was what?'

The noise came again, closer now: the sound of something big crashing through the trees.

'It's coming this way,' said Hereward.

'Look out!' Gwyneth's words were lost in a startled cry as a huge shape burst out from behind a bramble thicket, black against the white snow. It was a horse plunging in panic, its eyes rolling wildly and foam flecking its shoulders. It was saddled, but it had no rider; its reins flew free and it seemed a miracle that they had not already caught in the animal's hooves.

Gwyneth dived sideways, slipping in the powdery snow, and fell to her hands and knees. She caught a glimpse of Hereward leaping for the horse's head.

'Be careful!' she shouted.

Scrambling to her feet, she saw Hereward grasp one of the reins. The horse let out a loud whinny and reared up, carrying Hereward off his feet. When its hooves hit the ground again it charged forward, and dragged Hereward along for a few paces until a dense clump of hazel brought it up short. Half running, half sliding, he guided the horse around in a wide semi-circle and brought it to a standstill with its flanks heaving.

'God's bones!' Gwyneth gasped as she got a good look at the stallion for the first time. 'That's Father Godfrey's horse!'

Chapter Ten

'You're right!' said Hereward. 'I wonder what made it bolt?'

'And where is Father Godfrey?' added Gwyneth.

'We had better try and find him.'

Gwyneth was not at all sure about that suggestion. Certain as she was that Godfrey de Massard was M, she didn't want to be anywhere near him. But she realized that her brother was right. If the horse had thrown him, then he could be lying injured somewhere in the woods. A murderer should be made to account for his crimes, she thought. She was unwilling to admit to herself that she could not bear the thought of even a murderer left alone to die of cold.

Hereward looped the reins around the branch of a nearby tree. Giving the horse a final pat, he said, 'Stay there, lad. We'll come back for you.' Then he retrieved his axe and led the way down the trail that the horse had left through the snow.

Gwyneth fell in behind him. She was comforted by the thought that he was armed, even though she knew very well that her brother would be hard pressed to use the axe on anyone. Her throat was dry and she swallowed as she tried to imagine what they were going to find.

The stallion had left a swathe of trampled undergrowth and scattered snow and the trail was easy to follow as it looped around trees and bushes towards the river. Gwyneth and Hereward trod silently, their ears strained for any unusual sounds.

The first thing Gwyneth heard was a muffled shouting coming from somewhere ahead. Reaching out, she touched Hereward's arm and they both stopped to listen. Along with the shouting was a faint crackling.

'What's that?' Gwyneth whispered.

Hereward shook his head. 'I can't tell. Come on!'

The track led down to a small stream where the horse had smashed through a layer of ice, and up the slope on the other side. Gwyneth and Hereward leapt over the ice-strewn water and scrambled up the bank. As they came to the crest of the rise, Gwyneth saw bright flames leaping around an abandoned foresters' hut; the crackling sound came from sheaves of burning brushwood propped against the door. The shouting, louder now, came from behind the door.

Someone was trapped inside!

As she and Hereward ran forward she heard the crash of footsteps through the undergrowth and caught a glimpse of two men running away, clad in dark green tunics.

'That's Lady Isabelle's livery!' Gwyneth gasped. 'What are her servants doing out here?'

Hereward paid no attention. He darted round the corner of the hut where the flames had not yet reached and attacked the wooden wall with his axe. Splinters flew, but the planks were thick and resisted his attempts to break in. Gwyneth grabbed a branch and tried to rake the burning brushwood away from the door, but that side of the hut was well alight by now, the flames blazing up into the thatch. Ominously, the shouting had stopped.

She gave up and ran round to Hereward. As she reached him, she noticed a spot near the bottom of the wall where the wood was rotting away. 'Try there!' she cried, tugging at her brother's arm.

Hereward aimed his axe at the rotting wood. After only a few blows he managed to make a hole big enough to crawl through; still clutching the axe he dropped to his hands and knees and wriggled through.

Gwyneth followed him. Inside the hut, she could see nothing for swirling smoke that made her eyes water and caught in her throat. She tried to call out to Hereward but she could only cough.

Then a voice close beside her choked out, 'Here—be quick!'

Peering through her tears she made out the figure of Father Godfrey standing barely an arm's reach away. His wrists had been lashed together and bound to the post in the centre of the hut. The thatch above him was already burning, sending down sparks on his head and his woollen habit.

Gwyneth struggled to undo the knotted cords. 'Hereward!' she yelled, and doubled over in a fit of coughing.

Suddenly her brother was beside her. He sliced through the cords with one stroke of the axe against the wooden post. Father Godfrey pulled his hands free, swayed as if he was about to fall, and then grabbed Gwyneth and pushed her towards the gleam of snowlight that showed where the hole was.

'Out,' he rasped.

Gwyneth dropped to her knees and crawled through the gap, followed a moment later by Hereward. Last of all came Father Godfrey; he dragged himself a few paces away from the burning hut and collapsed face down in the snow.

As Gwyneth crouched beside him, shaking with a fear she had not felt inside the building, the roof of the hut fell in with a sigh and flames billowed up into the sky. She got to her feet, brushing snow and scraps of half-burnt straw from her skirt, and wiped her streaming eyes with her sleeve. Knowing how close she had come to a terrible death, she could do nothing but stare in silence at the flames.

Hereward came to stand beside her. 'If those really were Lady Isabelle's men,' he said in a hoarse whisper, 'they must have shut Father Godfrey in the hut and left him to burn. Why else would they have been running away?'

Gwyneth glanced down at the unmoving form of the priest. 'If Father Godfrey is indeed M, perhaps Lady Isabelle wanted to kill him to keep her part of the poisoning plot secret!'

Just then the priest groaned and sat up, rubbing his hands over his soot-stained face. His wrists were bleeding where he had wrenched at the cords in a vain attempt to free himself. With his tonsure on end and his eyes red and streaming, he had never looked less like the haughty aristocrat they had complained against in private so many times.

'Sir, are you all right?' she asked, dropping to her knees beside him, forgetting for a moment that he might be a cold-blooded murderer.

Father Godfrey coughed and took in a great gulp of air. 'I will be, in a moment.' Awkwardly he added, 'You have my thanks.'

'It was nothing,' said Hereward, looking equally embarrassed.

'But what happened, sir?' Gwyneth pressed daringly. 'Why did Lady Isabelle's men want to kill you?'

'You saw them?' For a moment Father Godfrey hesitated as if he was not sure how much to tell them. Then his mouth twisted in a grim line. 'Why should it surprise me, that the two of you are in the thick of this?'

For a moment Gwyneth felt hot with guilt, but

at least on this occasion they had been inno-
cently gathering firewood, not trying to interfere
in his investigation.

'I expect that I was getting too close to the
truth about that lady's activities,' the priest went
on. 'I have suspected for some time that she was
behind the poisoning at Dean Alexander's feast.'

'That's why she looked so frightened when she
met you at the abbey!' Hereward exclaimed.
'When you told her that you were investigating
the death of Nathaniel de Bere.'

Gwyneth flashed him a warning look. They
were not supposed to know that there was any
connection between Master de Bere and Lady
Isabelle Carfax. And from the sound of it, Father
Godfrey wasn't involved in the poisoning plot
himself, but had set out to investigate it.

Fortunately, Father Godfrey was too shaken
to realize that Hereward had given anything away.
'Why his death should concern her I do not
know,' he said, 'unless he was involved in the
plot too. But the lady clearly decided that I must
be disposed of before I learned anything more.
The letter you brought me was a request for a
meeting, here at this hut. She said that she had
valuable information to give me about Henry of

Truro.' Once more he rubbed his hands over his face. 'I was a fool to come alone,' he admitted.

'And then?' Hereward prompted.

'She and her servants were waiting for me. I fought, but her men were too strong for me.' The priest sounded ashamed that he had not managed to beat off his attackers. 'Lady Isabelle said I should pay the price for my interference. Then she left, and her men bound me inside the hut and set fire to it. I thought my hour had come, for I could not imagine that anyone would be in the woods in such weather as this.' He shivered.

Gwyneth and Hereward met each other's eyes. Gwyneth realized in dismay that if they had not been so sure that Father Godfrey was M, they might have shown him de Bere's hidden parchments by now, and he would not have risked his life by agreeing to meet Lady Isabelle alone.

'We were collecting firewood,' she explained, 'when your horse came crashing through the woods.'

'You found him!' Father Godfrey sat up straight, concern in every line of his face. 'If he's injured . . .'

'No, sir, he is well,' Hereward reassured him. 'We left him tied to a tree.'

'Then you deserve double thanks,' said Father Godfrey. He got to his feet, staggering a little. 'We had better go and collect him, and then I must speak with Master Thorson. He will arrest Lady Isabelle, I am sure.'

He stopped, head raised, listening. Gwyneth caught her breath as she heard something too: faint because of distance, but still unmistakable. It was the sound of a woman's screams.

Chapter Eleven

'Over there!' exclaimed Hereward. He set off at a run.

'Wait, boy!' Father Godfrey called, hurrying after him. 'You don't know what you will find.'

Gwyneth dashed after them, dragging her skirt away from tendrils of bramble that clutched at the wool. As the ground fell away into a steep slope dotted with trees, the screams grew louder; half-sliding, they plunged downwards and burst out of the trees into a clearing.

Not far away, a woman was struggling in the middle of a clump of thorns. Gwyneth's eyes stretched wide as she recognized Marion le Fevre. Her cloak and dress were caught up in the tangling branches, her face and hands bleeding where the thorns had scratched her. Beside her on the ground lay a tipped-over basket, with berries scattered around, blood-red against the snow.

'Oh, help, help!' Marion cried piteously. 'Please, someone help me!'

'Hold still,' Father Godfrey ordered, drawing a knife from his belt. 'We'll soon have you free.'

'No, no . . .' Mistress le Fevre did not seem at all reassured to see rescuers approaching. 'Over there,' she sobbed, trying to drag an arm free to point. 'Lady Isabelle . . . in the pool . . . Oh, God grant you are not too late!'

For the first time Gwyneth looked past the thorn thicket. At the foot of the slope was a smooth stretch of snow, broken at one point by a jagged hole revealing dark water.

'The ice broke . . . she fell . . .' Marion gasped.

'Stay here and help her,' Father Godfrey ordered, thrusting his knife into Hereward's hand before hurtling down the slope towards the hole in the ice.

A picture flashed into Gwyneth's mind of Lady Isabelle hurrying away from the forester's hut, looking over her shoulder, perhaps, to make sure that Father Godfrey had not escaped to pursue her. She would not have realized that the mantle of snow was covering a pool. A few steps onto the ice . . . the crack as it gave way beneath her weight . . .

Gwyneth shuddered. That was a death she would not have wished even on murderous Isabelle Carfax.

'I came to collect berries for dyeing my silks.' Marion was weeping more quietly now, standing still while Hereward cut away the thorns that were entangling her. 'I heard her cries and saw her struggling in the water, but the thorns caught me and I could not reach her. Then she vanished . . .'

Father Godfrey had reached the pool and was wading out into it. Gwyneth clasped her hands tight, hardly able to watch. Surely no one could swim for long in such bitter cold? The water had reached above the priest's waist when suddenly he plunged out of sight. Gwyneth barely had time to breathe a silent prayer before he reappeared, this time supporting a dark bundle in his arms, and floundered towards the bank. Lady Isabelle's head hung limply back at an impossible angle; she still wore the furred cloak and crimson velvet gown, heavy enough to drag her down in the icy water however desperately she fought to save herself.

Feeling sick, Gwyneth tore her gaze away and gave a hand to Marion le Fevre as Hereward slashed at the last of the thorns and the embroideress was freed. She clung to Gwyneth, still weeping; Gwyneth guided her gently to sit on a nearby tree-stump, and put an arm around her.

But Marion refused to be comforted. 'It's my fault,' she whispered. 'I should have done more.'

She glanced up as Godfrey de Massard came trudging up the slope. He looked exhausted and he was shivering like a drenched dog, his sodden habit clinging to him.

'Is she . . .' Marion ventured.

'Dead,' he answered heavily. 'We must take her body back to the village.'

Marion let out a little cry and broke into fresh sobs, burying her face in her hands. Even though Gwyneth felt sorry for her, she could not suppress a tiny stab of exasperation. Getting Mistress le Fevre home was going to be almost as difficult as transporting Lady Isabelle's lifeless body.

'We'll fetch your horse and our mule,' Hereward offered. 'Perhaps Mistress le Fevre could ride the mule, and you could carry Lady Isabelle on your horse.'

Father Godfrey nodded. 'Mistress le Fevre and I will wait here with her until you come back.'

'Stay with Father Godfrey,' Gwyneth said to

Marion, giving her an affectionate pat on the shoulder. 'We won't be long.'

As she followed Hereward back into the trees, she gave a last shocked look back at the dark waters of the pool, and the crimson stain of Lady Isabelle's gown spread out on the snow beside it.

The rest of the day passed in a blur and Gwyneth felt she had lived half a lifetime before she was able to curl up in bed, warm again and stuffed full of her mother's frumenty. Before she blew out the taper she looked across at her brother's bed, his body no more than a dark mound under the blankets.

'Hereward?'

'Hmm?'

'We were wrong about Father Godfrey. He isn't M after all. Oh, I'm so glad we didn't accuse him to Master Thorson!'

The only reply was a grunt.

'Hereward, listen! We have to decide what we're going to do tomorrow.'

Hereward let out a long sigh. His mop of chestnut hair emerged from the blankets as he raised himself on one elbow. 'What do you want to do?'

'I think we have to trust Father Godfrey. We know he can't be M, because if he was, Lady Isabelle wouldn't have tried to get rid of him.'

'Then who is M?'

Gwyneth shook her head impatiently. 'How do I know? Perhaps someone who followed Master de Bere from London? In any case, M might have killed Master de Bere because of what he knew about the poisoning plot, but he might just as easily have died because he was searching for the Holy Grail, and someone else wanted to find it first. M might not be involved at all.'

Her thoughts flew back to the ancient parchment that Wasim Kharab had translated, with its imperfect instructions about how to find the Grail, and to the two copper medallions, one discovered in the hole Master de Bere had dug at Chalcwelle, the other in the abbey infirmary. How were they connected, and had they really led to Master de Bere's death?

'Father Godfrey will never find out the truth unless we show him the parchments we found,' Hereward pointed out.

'I know.' Gwyneth swallowed nervously. 'He's going to be furious.'

'He can't do anything to us,' Hereward pointed out. 'We did save his life, after all.'

'Then you think we should take the parchments to him tomorrow?' Gwyneth asked, feeling a little encouraged as she realized her brother was right.

Hereward nodded.

'All right. We'll go and find him as soon as our morning tasks are done.'

Gwyneth blew out the taper and burrowed into her blankets but her mind would not rest easily after everything she had seen that day. As she closed her eyes and sank into sleep she seemed to hear the drowning cries of Lady Isabelle Carfax and see a swirl of dark water, blurring into a picture of the unmoving boots of Nathaniel de Bere.

Chapter Twelve

There was another heavy fall of snow during the night, so Gwyneth and Hereward had to start the day by helping Wat and Hankin dig a path from the inn door across the yard to the street. Most of the guests who were due to leave changed their minds and decided to stay on until the roads were clearer.

'It's a good thing the storeroom is well stocked,' Idony remarked at breakfast. 'As it is, they'll eat us out of house and home if the thaw doesn't come soon!'

Gwyneth smiled as she finished her bowl of warm oatmeal. Not long ago, her mother had been complaining that no one would come to the inn while a murderer was loose in Glastonbury.

When the snow was cleared, and Gwyneth and Hereward emerged into the street, they saw a solitary figure trudging past the market-place.

153

Gwyneth stared in surprise. 'Look, it's Ursus!' The hermit scarcely ever came into the village, and she wondered if he had been driven there by the harsh weather; his cell on the Tor, wherever it was, must be comfortless indeed in the bitter cold.

'Ursus, wait!' she called, picking up her skirt and floundering after him through the thick snow.

The hermit paused until she caught him up, though when she looked for his ready smile she found his face was grave, and she remembered again his strange behaviour when they had shown him the document written in ancient Arabic.

'Would you like to come and sit by our fire for a while?' she offered. 'I know mother and father would welcome you.'

A smile reached his eyes, and he suddenly looked more like the Ursus she was used to. 'I thank you, but no,' he replied. 'I must return to the Tor.'

'Then take some food with you,' said Hereward. 'Mother is baking bread—I'll fetch you some.' Without waiting for a reply, he sped back to the Crown.

'That is kind,' Ursus said, bowing his head. With a searching look at Gwyneth, he asked,

'Did you manage to read the parchment you showed me?'

Gwyneth's nervousness returned. 'Yes,' she replied hesitantly. 'We met Wasim Kharab at the market in Wells, and he told us what it said. It . . . it gave instructions about how to find the Holy Grail.'

Ursus's eyes narrowed. 'So Master de Bere was digging for the prize esteemed by Christian men above all others? Then he was a bold man— or a greedy one.'

Gwyneth was a little shocked that the hermit showed no surprise at her news that the Grail might be hidden so close to Glastonbury, and she began to wonder if he had already known what the parchment had to tell. Before he could say anything else, Hereward came panting up with a couple of loaves wrapped in a linen cloth.

'Here,' he said, thrusting them into Ursus's hands. 'Mother says you're to come to the inn if you want more.'

'Then thank her for her gracious kindness,' said Ursus. To Gwyneth, he said quietly, 'There is a time for all things to be found, my child, but some things need to stay hidden. Remember that when you go seeking.' Without waiting for a reply he turned and strode away down the street towards the Tor.

'What was that about?' said Hereward, staring after him.

'I told him Wasim Kharab read the parchment for us,' Gwyneth replied. 'He acted strangely, as if he already knew what it says.'

'Then perhaps he knew how to read it all along,' he suggested, echoing Gwyneth's earlier thoughts.

'But that means he lied to us when we showed it to him!' she protested. 'Ursus wouldn't do that.'

'He would, if he's M,' Hereward reminded her.

Gwyneth wanted to insist that their friend could not possibly be a cold-hearted murderer, but the words died on her lips. Ursus's behaviour had been too strange. Even if he was not M, he had some other secret that he was hiding from them.

'He helped us before,' she began.

A cold, wet blow in the middle of her back interrupted her. She whirled round to see Ivo and Amabel Thorson standing on the edge of the market-place. Amabel was doubled over with laughter; Ivo hurled another snowball which caught Hereward full in the face.

'I'll pay you for that!' Hereward yelled, bending down to scoop up a handful of snow.

A moment later snowballs were flying across the street, some slapping against the walls of the shops behind them, others meeting their target to provoke a startled yelp. Gwyneth's hands tingled with cold as she hurled the tightly-packed snow at her friends, and she ducked quickly to avoid a missile flying at her from Amabel's hands.

At once a bellow sounded from behind her. 'Young ruffians! I'll speak to your father about this!'

Gwyneth spun round to see Rhys Freeman, his hair and beard soaking from Amabel's bursting snowball and his face red with anger.

'We're sorry, Master Freeman!' Ivo called out. 'We didn't see you there!'

He and Amabel exchanged a glance, their eyes sparkling; clearly they were not sorry at all. They burst out laughing again and ran up the street. Rhys Freeman blundered after them, slipped, and fell full length in the snow.

Hereward clapped a hand over his mouth, and Gwyneth had to work hard to keep a straight face as she and Hereward went to help Master Freeman up.

'Young ruffians,' he grumbled as he brushed snow off himself. 'If I were their father I'd take a belt to them.' Still grumbling, he retreated into his shop.

'And never a word of thanks to us,' said Hereward.

'Do you expect thanks from Master Freeman?' Gwyneth shook the clinging snow from her skirt. 'Come on, let's ask mother if we may go to the abbey. It's time to take the parchments to Father Godfrey.'

Gwyneth and Hereward reached the abbey in time to see the monks leaving the chapel after terce. They waited close to the entrance until they saw Godfrey de Massard walking beside Brother Barnabas.

The priest looked pale and tired after his ordeal the day before, and as he gestured in his discussion with the abbey steward, the sleeve of his habit fell back to reveal a bandage on his wrist.

Feeling anxious at the thought of what they had to show to him, Gwyneth stepped forward. 'Father Godfrey, may we speak to you?'

The priest looked surprised, but he managed

a small smile. 'Of course.' Murmuring a farewell to Brother Barnabas, he indicated the stone bench inside the Lady Chapel porch. 'Shall we sit here?'

Clasping her hands tightly in front of her, Gwyneth said, 'We have something to show you, Father.'

Godfrey de Massard seated himself next to her and Hereward took the place on his other side, drawing the sheaf of parchments out of his tunic. 'We discovered these,' he said, swallowing nervously. 'They belonged to Nathaniel de Bere.'

Father Godfrey's eyes gleamed as he reached for the parchments. 'Where did you find them?'

'Among his things,' Gwyneth confessed.

'Some hidden in his room,' Hereward added, 'and some stitched into his horse's saddle-cloth.'

'Then he tried to conceal them,' Father Godfrey commented. He began to leaf through the sheets, but just when Gwyneth thought they might have escaped more questioning he stopped and asked more harshly, 'How long have you had these?'

Gwyneth glanced at her brother, searching for an answer that would not bring down the priest's fury on them. Hereward opened his mouth but nothing came out. Their silence was guilty in itself; Godfrey de Massard's eyes grew cold as ice and his mouth tightened with anger.

'For several days, I take it,' he snapped. 'Since you first brought me his possessions. Have you no sense at all?' His voice rose and he paused, clearly trying to control his anger. 'Did you take no notice when I told you not to interfere? Dean Alexander and his guests were almost poisoned. Nathaniel de Bere is dead. I almost died yesterday!' He broke off, shaking his head.

'We're sorry,' Gwyneth ventured.

'Sorry?' Father Godfrey's voice was scathing. 'I should have been sorry if I had had to speak to your parents of your death. How often must I tell you that these are not matters for children?'

Gwyneth remembered that he had said much the same on the day when he came to the Crown to ask for Nathaniel de Bere's things. Then she had been angry at his arrogance; now she realized that he was genuinely concerned for them. Her understanding made her feel even worse; there was nothing she and Hereward could say to excuse themselves.

With a final exasperated snort, Father Godfrey turned back to the parchments, beginning with

Nicholas de Bere's letter and his will. His eyes widened when he came to the scrap of parchment from Lady Isabelle Carfax, making the appointment to meet Master de Bere at the Crown.

'Lady Isabelle's seal!' he breathed, half to himself. He lifted his gaze to Gwyneth and Hereward. 'Dean Alexander asked me to investigate the attempt to poison him and his guests. I suspected that Henry of Truro was at the bottom of it, and that Father Aidan, King Richard's favourite priest, was his real target. Dean Alexander dismissed his cook—there was no real evidence against him, but clearly he could not be trusted—and my men informed me that he went straight to Lady Isabelle. That alone made me sure that she was involved, but I had no other proof.'

'So that's why Lady Isabelle looked afraid when she heard you were investigating Nathaniel de Bere's death!' Hereward exclaimed. 'She would be worried that you would discover the blackmail, and her part in the poisoning plot.'

'Indeed.' Father Godfrey read her note again. 'Yet there is little enough evidence here—not enough to call her to account for her crime had she still been alive.'

Gwyneth shivered. Lady Isabelle had paid the price for everything that she had done and more. 'She must have been afraid that M would kill her, too,' she murmured. 'But in the end, she died by accident.'

'Yes, Mistress le Fevre can witness to that,' said Hereward, and added daringly, 'Unless she killed Lady Isabelle herself. She looked angry enough, when they met at the Crown!'

'Don't be stupid!' Anger spurted up inside Gwyneth at the thought of accusing the embroideress of such a terrible crime. 'No one commits murder because they have to change to another bedchamber!'

Hereward muttered an apology. 'Weren't you afraid the poisoners would try again?' he asked Father Godfrey, changing the subject.

The priest shook his head. 'Father Aidan was due to leave for the Holy Land with letters for the king. That is why I believed that the plot was directed against him. If Henry could have put his own man in his place it would have been an ideal way to spy on King Richard . . . perhaps even another plot to assassinate him.'

'So the poisoners only had that one chance,' Hereward said. 'After that, Father Aidan had gone.'

'Exactly,' replied Father Godfrey. 'God be thanked that he is safe.'

'There's a letter from another priest,' Gwyneth pointed out. 'He must have been the man who would have taken Father Aidan's place.'

Father Godfrey leafed through the parchments again and found Father Herbert's letter. 'This man was afraid of M too,' he remarked. 'And with good cause. Nicholas de Bere died and so did his brother, and we cannot blame Lady Isabelle for either of those deaths. She never went to London, and she had no reason to want Nicholas dead. And although Nathaniel de Bere was blackmailing her, she did not arrive in Glastonbury until after he was killed.'

'Do you think M killed Nathaniel?' Gwyneth asked.

'It is possible.' A reluctant smile tugged at Father Godfrey's mouth. 'Did you never consider that I might be M?' he asked. 'Coming from Wells as I do . . .'

Gwyneth felt herself going red.

'You, Father Godfrey?' Hereward said quickly. 'No, we never suspected you—did we, Gwyneth?'

'The thought never entered our heads,' Gwyneth assured the priest.

Father Godfrey's mouth twitched again and he gave them a searching look, as if he did not entirely believe them, but he said nothing more. Instead, he turned to the last document, the parchment written in Arabic. 'So this is what Father Herbert said was so precious,' he commented. 'I wish that I could read it and find out why.'

'We can tell you, sir,' Hereward said. At Father Godfrey's look of surprise he added, 'You remember Wasim Kharab, the Moorish merchant?'

Father Godfrey nodded. 'Another of Henry of Truro's men. He sold Master Freeman's relics to fund Henry's campaign.'

'We met him the day we went to Wells,' Gwyneth explained. 'He read the parchment for us.'

'Really? What did it say?'

'It was written by one of the companions of Joseph of Arimathea,' said Hereward. 'It gives instructions about how to find the Holy Grail.'

Father Godfrey's brows shot up and he dropped the parchment to make the sign of the cross. 'The Holy Grail?' His voice shook, but he recovered himself almost at once. 'Then that is why Nathaniel de Bere was digging at Chalcwelle!'

'Yes, sir,' said Gwyneth, 'but he would never have found the Grail. Wasim said that the parchment only gives half the directions, and that somewhere there must be another one.'

Father Godfrey nodded. 'That makes sense,' he said, 'for if the Grail is truly buried at Chalcwelle, it would not reveal itself to wicked men.' For a moment he looked out of the porch, his gaze drifting unfocused over the snowy ground. 'If only you had shown me this sooner! It gives us a completely different reason for Nathaniel de Bere's death. Perhaps he was killed by someone who wanted to steal the Grail, quite separate from the poisoning.'

'He wouldn't have shown the parchment to anyone else,' Hereward pointed out.

'No, but Father Herbert knew about it—' Godfrey de Massard touched the priest's letter—'and who knows how many people he told? This gives a whole new turn to my investigation.'

He was gathering the documents together, ready to rise, when a shadow fell across them. Gwyneth looked up to see Brother Timothy standing in the entrance to the porch. His gaze fell on the parchments Father Godfrey was holding, and for a moment his eyes opened wide, as if there was something there he recognized.

Only a flash, and then it was gone, and Brother Timothy was asking urgently, 'Have you seen Brother Peter? Did he go into the chapel?'

Father Godfrey shook his head. Hereward said, 'I thought Brother Peter was still in the infirmary?'

'He is. He should be.' Brother Timothy twisted his hands together. 'But when I went to visit him just now he was not there, and Brother Padraig did not see him leave.'

'Is he not in his cell?' Father Godfrey prompted. 'Have you looked?'

'Yes, but he isn't there either.' Brother Timothy's voice grew louder in his agitation. 'He has disappeared!'

Chapter Thirteen

Father Godfrey rose to his feet. 'We must find him at once. Brother Peter is unwell. He cannot be left to wander by himself in this foul weather.'

'Brother Padraig is organizing a search,' said Brother Timothy.

'Then I will go and help him.' Still grasping the documents, Father Godfrey gave Gwyneth and Hereward a curt nod of farewell and hurried off towards the infirmary.

Brother Timothy let out a long sigh and rubbed his hands over his face. Gwyneth thought that he looked weary to the bone, as if some great burden had been placed upon him.

'Do you have any idea where Brother Peter might have gone?' she asked.

'There is one thought in my mind.' To Gwyneth's surprise, Brother Timothy did not sound relieved at the prospect of finding the old man. 'He may have left the abbey altogether, and if so, I know what his purpose might have been. Will you come with me to search for him?'

Gwyneth exchanged a doubtful look with Hereward. Brother Timothy's behaviour had been strange ever since the discovery of Nathaniel de Bere's body, and her stomach gave an uneasy twist at the thought of being alone with him. Then a wave of guilt washed over her. How could she have been so suspicious of a friend she had known all her life?

'Yes, of course we will,' she said, and Hereward nodded agreement.

But her old fears flocked back like soot-winged crows when Brother Timothy led them across the abbey grounds and out through the back gate. He was leading them back up to Chalcwelle.

Snow lay thickly on the path as they left the last houses behind, disturbed only by the tracks of animals or birds. Gwyneth had to lift her skirt clear, but the drifts came over the tops of her boots, soaking her feet with icy snow-water.

A deep silence covered the woodland. Not even a bird sang. The sound of their footsteps was muffled, so that all Gwyneth could hear was her own breathing and her heartbeat pounding in her ears.

At last the silence was broken by the trickling of water as the path joined the stream from Chalcwelle. Ice fringed its edges, but in the centre the water still flowed. Its red colour was stark against the white blanket of snow, though it would never again be as deeply scarlet as when the blood of Nathaniel de Bere had stained it.

When they reached the bottom of the slope which led up to the spring, Brother Timothy did not pause to catch his breath but began to climb, grim-faced. Gwyneth and Hereward clawed their way up after him in a shower of snow until they came to the rock face where the spring rose.

The tiny cave was clear of all but a dusting of snow, the water welling steadily from the crack in the rock. At first Gwyneth could see no sign of Brother Peter there, until a familiar voice said, 'Be welcome.'

She spun round to see Ursus standing a few paces away, near the hole that Nathaniel de Bere had begun to dig. Huddled on the ground at his feet was the body of the old monk, and beside him lay a spade. Snow had been scraped away from the pile of earth as if someone had been trying to fill in the hole.

At first Gwyneth could not speak. Terror held

her in a grip as cold as ice. The evidence before her told her that Ursus had struck him down, and if that were true, he must also be the murderer of Nathaniel de Bere.

Ursus turned a sprig of the Glastonbury thorn between his fingers, the fragile white flowers newly opened. 'I knew that you would come,' he said to Brother Timothy.

'Of course.' Brother Timothy bowed, and Gwyneth caught for a moment on his face a look of the deepest awe. The air seemed to tingle with secrets.

'Do you two know each other?' Hereward blurted out in surprise, breaking the spell.

'We have not met until now,' Ursus replied. 'But yes, you might say that we know each other.' He offered no more explanation, and Gwyneth and Hereward did not dare ask.

Brother Timothy knelt beside Brother Peter and raised him up, cradling his head and shoulders. Gwyneth realized that the old monk was not dead. His eyelids flickered, and his chest heaved with the effort to find breath.

'I found him lying here,' said Ursus. 'Listen with compassion to what he tells you. He is a good man. And remember that even though nothing stays lost for ever, some things are best left unlooked for.'

Bending down, he placed the sprig of Glastonbury thorn in Brother Peter's fingers and rested his hand briefly on the old monk's head. 'Thank you, old friend,' he said. 'May God receive you into His peace.' Then he straightened up and walked away down the hill.

Brother Timothy pulled off his cloak and wrapped it around Brother Peter. 'Lie still, Brother,' he urged. 'Gwyneth and Hereward will help me carry you back to the abbey. We'll soon have you warm in the infirmary again.'

'No—wait, I must speak.' Brother Peter's voice quivered with age and weakness. Gwyneth felt uncomfortable. If Brother Peter was about to make his final confession, she and Hereward should not be there to hear it.

'My sins are heavy on me,' the monk went on. 'God knows I did not seek the man's death when I found him digging here. But it was my hand that struck him down.'

Gwyneth pressed a hand to her mouth to keep back a cry of surprise. Was the old man confessing to the murder of Nathaniel de Bere? There was no possibility that the gentle monk could be M, the powerful traitor behind the failed poisoning plot. The cause of de Bere's death must have something to do with the hidden Grail after all.

'I begged him to stop what he was doing. He was wrong to look for such a holy thing.' Brother Peter's eyes were wide open now, gazing in front of him with an expression of anguish as if he was reliving that terrible day. 'I told him it was not the time for the Grail to be revealed. But he laughed at me, and when I pleaded with him again he came at me with the spade.' Breathless, the old monk had to break off.

Gwyneth felt tears of compassion hot on her cheek. Nathaniel de Bere had died because of his quest for treasure on the Glastonbury hillside, and once more Brother Peter had taken it upon himself to protect that treasure's hiding place. When Arthur's coffin had first been uncovered, Brother Peter had stolen the cross that had been buried with it in order to keep the bones of the great king from being displayed to the world. He had been desperate to guard the relics from covetous eyes, and give Arthur some privacy in a secret grave.

Brother Timothy's eyes were dark with grief. Gwyneth waited for him to tell her and Hereward to leave, but instead he looked down at the old monk again. 'Peace, Brother,' he murmured. 'If you have the strength, tell us the rest of what happened.'

'I tried to grab the spade from him,' the weak voice continued. 'Only to defend myself. But he was stronger . . . we wrestled, and then he wrenched the spade from me. He would have struck me but he slipped and fell on the spade. The sharp edge of the metal cleft his head.' A dry sob shook the old man's frail body. 'So much blood, flowing into the spring, turning the water scarlet . . .'

'You did not strike him,' Brother Timothy reassured him. 'You are guiltless of his death.'

Brother Peter shook his head. 'If I had never come here, if I had not spoken, he would live still.'

'To do greater wickedness,' said Brother Timothy.

'Yes,' Gwyneth put in. 'He was a blackmailer, Brother Peter. An evil man.'

Brother Peter's gaze flickered towards her and away again, to rest on the white thorn blossoms that he still held in his hand. He smiled faintly and let out a little sigh, and his head slipped to one side.

'Is he dead?' Gwyneth whispered, though even as she asked the question she made out the faint rise and fall of the old man's chest, and heard his shallow, rasping breaths.

'No.' Brother Timothy looked up with tears on his face. 'But he is very ill. Come, help me carry him back to the abbey.'

'But how did he know that Master de Bere would be here, digging up the Grail?' Hereward asked as Brother Timothy folded his cloak more tightly around the old monk.

Brother Timothy shook his head. 'You heard what he told us. You know as much as I. Come, help me lift him.' He looked from Hereward to Gwyneth and back again, smiling sadly. 'Soon all questions will be answered.'

Chapter Fourteen

'I wonder how Brother Peter is?' Gwyneth puffed. She and Hereward set down Mistress le Fevre's chest of fabrics in its old place in the best bedchamber, and she straightened up in relief, rubbing her back. 'There's been no news from the abbey.'

'When we've finished this, we'll ask mother if we can visit him,' Hereward said.

It was the morning after their startling discovery at Chalcwelle. In spite of their anxiety about Brother Peter, Gwyneth and Hereward had been kept busy with tasks around the inn, and there had been no chance to find the answers to the thousand questions that still tormented them. They knew at last how Nathaniel de Bere had died—because he was looking for the Holy Grail rather than because he had tried to blackmail the people who had been involved in the poisoning plot. But they were still no nearer to discovering the identity of the mysterious and much-feared M.

'There!' said Gwyneth, surveying the room. 'That's done.'

Lady Isabelle Carfax's belongings had been packed away, ready for her family to claim them when they came from Wells to arrange her funeral. Marion le Fevre's belongings had been restored to their place, and a bright fire burnt in the hearth. Lamps were lit and the shutters barred against the cold.

'It's wonderful,' said a voice from the door. 'Thank you so much. It's as if I'd never been away.'

Gwyneth turned to see Mistress le Fevre standing with one hand on the door frame as she looked around her bedchamber. The day before, she had kept to her bed to recover from her ordeal, and even now Gwyneth thought she looked pale and fragile, with scratches from the thorns still visible on her hands and face.

'Do you want to go back to bed, mistress?' Gwyneth asked anxiously. 'I'll ask mother for a hot brick.'

'Goodness, no, child!' Marion le Fevre laughed lightly. 'I must return to my work.' Her laughter died as she added, 'Though it will be long before I forget that dreadful day.'

'We won't forget it either,' Hereward said, and Gwyneth agreed, shivering at the memory of the blazing hut and Lady Isabelle's body stretched out in the snow.

Just then she heard the inn door open and close, and Ivo and Amabel Thorson's voices rising from the foot of the stairs.

'Call if you want anything, mistress,' she said with a quick curtsy, and with Hereward just behind her she went to find their friends.

When she reached the passage below she saw the twins standing just inside the door, their faces glowing pink from the cold.

'We've a message from father,' Ivo announced. 'Really it's for Master Mason, but you can tell him if you like.'

'What is it?' asked Hereward.

'Father is closing the investigation into Master de Bere's death,' Amabel told them. 'He had a long talk with Father Godfrey yesterday, and he thinks that the murderer must have left the village.'

'Probably gone back to London, he said,' Ivo added.

Gwyneth exchanged a glance with her brother. Only they and Brother Timothy knew that the man responsible for Nathaniel de Bere's death was still in the abbey, and they would never tell anyone. It was not as if Brother Peter was dangerous to anyone else; he had not meant to kill, and the merchant's death had been an accident brought on by de Bere's own greed. Gwyneth wondered briefly if Father Godfrey had told Finn Thorson the truth, and the two men had agreed that it was best for everyone in Glastonbury to believe they were safe because the murderer was a stranger long gone.

'Master de Bere's wife has sent servants to bring his body home for burial,' Ivo went on, 'but father said they had to leave his horse. You can keep that in payment of Master de Bere's bill.'

Hereward's eyes gleamed at the thought of the fine horse staying in the stable at the Crown, though he looked downcast a moment later when Gwyneth warned, 'Don't get your hopes up. You know that father will sell it at the next horse fair. We've no use for a horse like that.'

Hereward nodded resignedly.

Ivo and Amabel said goodbye and were going

out again when Amabel turned back. 'I almost forgot! We met Brother Timothy on our way here. He asked us to tell you to meet him at Chalcwelle when terce is over.'

Something between excitement and dread bubbled up inside Gwyneth. She had been expecting a message from Brother Timothy, but only with news of whether Brother Peter was getting better. She did not know why he should ask them to go to Chalcwelle.

She and Hereward hurried into the kitchen, where Idony Mason was chopping herbs for soup, and Gwyneth passed on Brother Timothy's request.

'May we go, mother?' Hereward asked.

'Of course, if the holy brother asks it,' said Idony. 'But you've time to go and collect the eggs first, and Gwyneth, there's a batch of bread ready for kneading.'

When their tasks were done, Gwyneth and Hereward hurried up Tor Lane towards Chalcwelle. A soft wind stirred the powdery surface of the snow, and all around them was the constant pattering of water drops as the icicles hanging from the trees began to melt. A thaw was coming, and for now the bitter weather was growing kinder.

Brother Timothy was seated on a rock just inside the cave where the spring bubbled up. A few paces away the hermit Ursus was shovelling earth and snow back into the hole Nathaniel de Bere had dug, and Brother Peter had started to fill in.

One look at Brother Timothy's face showed Gwyneth that he had grave news.

'Brother Peter . . .' she began.

'He died early this morning,' Brother Timothy told her. Gwyneth felt tears hot in her eyes; the young monk rose and laid a hand on her shoulder. 'Do not grieve,' he said. 'He was old and tired, and now he is with God. Before he died he confessed his sins to Abbot Henry, and the abbot absolved him. He died at peace.'

Remembering the torment the old man had been suffering when she saw him last, Gwyneth felt relieved for one comfort at least, but she still wished that he might have recovered.

'He wasn't a murderer,' Hereward said stoutly, blinking several times.

'No, he was not,' Brother Timothy agreed.

Returning to his seat, and gesturing for them to join him in the cave, he went on, 'You have discovered so much, I think the time has come for me to tell you the rest, so that you can understand who Brother Peter was and why he acted as he did.'

Curiosity flared in Gwyneth like a flame. She took a seat close by Brother Timothy, with Hereward on his other side, and leaned forward eagerly to listen. Ursus drove his spade into the ground and came to stand nearby, gazing out over the woodland towards the massive shape of the Tor. He scarcely seemed to listen, and Gwyneth suddenly suspected that he already knew what Brother Timothy was going to say.

'The old tales tell us that many of the treasures of King Arthur are hidden in and around Glastonbury, once the Isle of Avalon,' Brother Timothy began.

'Arthur's bones, and the cross,' said Hereward. 'And the Holy Grail.'

'And—' Gwyneth stopped herself from telling the monk about the cave of sleeping warriors, which she and Hereward had entered with Bedwyn, the silent stonemason. If Brother

Timothy did not know about it, perhaps she should keep its secret.

Brother Timothy nodded, seeming not to notice her hesitation. 'Through all the years since Arthur's reign, a line of Protector monks have guarded the treasures. Not just here in Glastonbury, but all over Britain and beyond, to make sure they should not be revealed until the time was right. They have served faithfully year after year with little thanks, for their work has to be secret.'

'Great evil would arise,' Ursus put in unexpectedly, turning to look at Gwyneth and Hereward, 'if such precious, powerful things were revealed before their time.'

'That's why Brother Peter stole the cross!' Hereward realized out loud. 'He said all along that he wanted Arthur's bones to be left undisturbed. And why he tried so hard to protect the Grail from Nathaniel de Bere.'

'This is true,' said Brother Timothy. 'Alas for Brother Peter, he grew so old and his wits became so confused that he was no longer equal to the heavy task laid on him. He did not see that the time had come for King Arthur's bones and the cross to reappear in the world. When he heard that Nathaniel de Bere was digging here at Chalcwelle, he came straightway to stop him, knowing that he could be looking for one treasure alone.'

'He judged rightly in one thing,' Ursus murmured. 'It is not time for the Grail to be revealed.'

'We saw him leave the abbcy!' Gwyneth remembered the morning she and Hereward had brought breakfast to the workmen when Brother Peter had almost collided with them in the darkness of the gateway. 'That's why he looked so upset.'

'But how did he know about Master de Bere?' Hereward asked curiously.

'The firewood seller told him,' Brother Timothy replied. 'He had been up here collecting wood, and saw Nathaniel de Bere digging.' With a sad smile he added, 'The pedlar thought it was no more than a good piece of gossip—a madman in fine gold boots digging on the hillside so early.'

'So you followed Brother Peter,' said Gwyneth, beginning to piece together what had happened on the morning of Nathaniel de Bere's death.

'I knew nothing of the pedlar until Brother Peter told me yesterday,' the monk went on. 'But when there was no sign of Brother Peter at breakfast, I suspected where he might have gone. I came looking for him, and found you here instead.'

'And Master de Bere's body . . .' Gwyneth murmured.

'The thought that he had caused a death tortured Brother Peter,' the young monk explained to her. 'He could not bear to think of what he had done, and his mind at last gave way. God be praised that it cleared again at the very end so that he could make his final confession.'

'How do you know all this, Brother Timothy?' asked Hereward. 'If the Protector monks work in secret?'

Brother Timothy smiled, suddenly reminding Gwyneth of the young boy who had bettered all others in tree-climbing. 'Have you not guessed? I am the next in the line of Protectors. Brother Peter passed his duty on to me.' From the front of his habit he drew out a fine chain; on the end of it was a copper medallion in the shape of a scarlet teardrop. 'You have seen this before, I think.'

'In the infirmary!' Hereward gasped.

'Indeed. It is the sign worn by all the Protector

monks. Brother Peter tried to give it to me on his sick bed, and dropped it. I could not find it easily, and could not search the room while the others were there.' He shook his head, half exasperated. 'It would be you who found it, Hereward! I did not know what to say to you, for how could I explain all this?'

'If you had, Hereward might have told you something else,' Gwyneth said, with a glimmer of satisfaction that Brother Timothy was not the only one with secrets to reveal. 'Show him, Hereward.'

Her brother opened up his pouch and brought out the medallion they had discovered in the hole Nathaniel de Bere had dug. Gwyneth watched Brother Timothy's eyes widen in amazement, and felt glad that they had forgotten to hand the teardrop over to Father Godfrey when they gave him the documents.

Brother Timothy stared at the scarlet drop on Hereward's palm. 'Where did you get it?'

As quickly as she could Gwyneth explained how Father Herbert had sent both the medallion and the parchment to Nathaniel de Bere in an attempt to pay off the man who had threatened to reveal his part in the poisoning plot.

'Father Herbert must have been another Protector.' Brother Timothy frowned. 'It was a grievous sin for him to give up his trust to a wicked man.'

'He did not.' Ursus took the medallion from Hereward's hand. 'He tricked de Bere, for the parchment gave only half the instructions of how to find the Grail. Without the other, it was useless. Father Herbert may have been in fear of his life or his reputation, but he kept faith as well as he could.'

Gwyneth stared at him. She had been right that Ursus had known all along what the parchment was.

The hermit met her gaze, and the old, kind smile reappeared. 'Forgive me, Gwyneth,' he said, as if he could read her mind. 'The parchment could have placed you in great danger, and the less you knew of it the better.'

Gwyneth was not entirely sure that she agreed but she did not argue. She was too relieved to have her old friend Ursus back again, free of all the suspicion that had gathered around him.

'You gave this parchment to Father Godfrey de Massard,' Brother Timothy went on.

'Yes,' said Gwyneth. 'I thought you recognized

it, when you saw him with it in the chapel porch.'

The monk nodded. 'I had never seen it before, but Brother Peter had described it to me, with the other treasures of Arthur that now are in my care. It is dangerous indeed.'

Ursus had turned away to gaze across the hillside once more; now he said calmly, 'The priest comes.'

Gwyneth sprang to her feet, but she could see and hear nothing and she wondered how Ursus could possibly know.

'I asked Father Godfrey to come,' said Brother Timothy, 'and to bring the parchment. It is time to make an end.'

Ursus nodded gravely and bowed. 'I will say farewell. I am not needed here.'

Gwyneth opened her mouth to protest—he seemed to know more about these secrets than anyone—but before she could speak, the hermit had slipped away. Moments later she heard the sound of someone climbing the slope. Godfrey de Massard's tall, dark-robed figure appeared and strode across the open ground towards them.

'You asked to meet me, Brother,' he said, addressing the monk. 'Could we not have spoken together at the abbey?'

Brother Timothy rose from his seat. 'No, Father,' he replied. 'What is to be done must happen here. Did you bring the parchment with you?'

For answer, Godfrey de Massard drew the Arabic document out of his habit. The drawing of the scarlet teardrop looked to Gwyneth like a spot of blood, and she could not help remembering how much blood had been spilled by evil men in their greed to lay hands on the Grail.

'What do you want with it?' the priest asked.

'I want to destroy it,' Brother Timothy replied.

Father Godfrey took a step back. 'But it's evidence!'

'Of what?' Brother Timothy challenged mildly. 'It will tell you nothing about the evil men you seek, and if it survives it will draw still more men into wickedness. The Holy Grail is not a treasure to be sold in the market-place, and this is not the time for it to be revealed.'

He spoke with authority and Gwyneth realized that her old friend had grown, almost overnight, into a man of greater wisdom than she would ever have thought possible. Even Father Godfrey seemed to be aware of it; at least, he did not argue any longer, though he looked reluctant as he laid the parchment in Brother Timothy's hands.

'What about M?' Hereward blurted out suddenly.

Father Godfrey turned to look at him. 'M?' he echoed.

'The person who arranged the poisoning plot in the first place,' Gwyneth explained. 'We . . . we know because of what the letters said. M contacted the other people—the priest at Smithfield, the apothecary Nicholas de Bere, and Lady Isabelle—and charged them with their roles. It seemed logical that Nathaniel de Bere might have blackmailed M too, and been murdered to keep him silent once and for all.'

'As you know, we thought at first that M was the murderer,' Hereward put in. 'But it seems not, now that we know de Bere died by accident. And there's nothing in the parchments to tell us who M might have been.'

Father Godfrey looked from one to the other. 'You have clearly been spending as much thought as I on these crimes,' he remarked drily. 'You are right, we are no closer to learning the identity of this M than when de Bere first arrived in Glastonbury. But I think we can assume that it is no one from this village, and this is a plot that was begun far away—perhaps even in Wales, where Henry of Truro builds his armies again.'

Hereward raised his eyebrows at Gwyneth to draw attention to the way Father Godfrey seemed to be blaming Henry of Truro yet again for misadventures close to their home.

As if he could tell what they were thinking, Father Godfrey's mouth twisted in a smile and he raised one hand. 'I know that King Richard has many enemies as well as Henry of Truro, but the threat from this man cannot be taken lightly. Like a wolf, he sleeps with one eye open, waiting for a chance to strike again.'

Gwyneth shivered and drew her cloak closer around her shoulders. Seeing that she was chilled to the bone, Brother Timothy held up the parchment that Father Godfrey had handed to him. 'We have one more task before we can go home.'

He crouched down with his mud-stained robe tucked around his bony ankles; Gwyneth and Hereward knelt beside him to watch, and Father Godfrey stood a little distance away, watching them with his eyes narrowed above the handsome cheekbones.

Gwyneth knew Brother Timothy was right to

destroy the parchment, however ancient and sacred it was. The second parchment, with the other half of the instructions, would be useless without it and the Holy Grail would be safe until the time came for it to reappear in the world. And then, she trusted, it would need no map in order to be found.

Brother Timothy scooped a shallow hole in the snow, crumpled the parchment and laid it down. Then he took a flint from his pouch and struck a spark. The document caught; a brown spot spread across the yellowing parchment and a thin thread of smoke rose wavering into the air. A moment later, scarlet and orange flame sprang up in a greedy, hissing tongue; the words that would have guided seekers of the Grail were lost as the parchment blackened.

Gwyneth cast a swift glance at the two clerics. Brother Timothy's face was calm and intent, as if he gazed into a world she could not see. Godfrey de Massard simply looked bemused.

The flames died. The parchment crumbled into a fine white ash, and the wind began to blow it away, dusting the waters of the spring with a few tiny glittering motes. The stream carried the ash swiftly away, just as it had washed away the blood of Nathaniel de Bere. The merchant had come to Glastonbury in search of holy treasure won by blackmail and threats, and had died in an accident that had set Hereward and Gwyneth looking for murderers among those they knew best and longest.

The last of the fragments vanished into the red-tinged spring, and to Gwyneth it seemed as if the troubled memories of the dead had been carried away with it, leaving only the silent wood covered in clean, white snow.

Other books in the series:

The Buried Cross
ISBN 0 19 275362 2

Gwyneth and Hereward Mason witness a marvellous discovery deep below the abbey courtyard. Could this cross found near the oak-tree coffin really prove that these are the bones of the legendary King Arthur?

Disaster strikes —the relics have gone! Gwyneth and Hereward *must* find them in order to save the abbey's fortunes. A sinister priest, a mysterious hermit, and a sneaky merchant all seem to have a part to play in the disappearance.

Just how far will Gwyneth and Hereward have to go to solve the mystery . . . ?

The Silent Man
ISBN 0 19 275363 0

Where is Eleanor? When the little girl goes missing, the whole of Glastonbury sets about trying to find her. Then suspicion falls on Bedwyn, the shy mute working on the abbey, and he's seized and thrown into jail.

Gwyneth and Hereward are sure that Bedwyn would never hurt anyone. But he can't speak up for himself so they must try to prove his innocence.

With the help of Ursus the hermit, Gwyneth and Hereward begin to piece together the clues to Eleanor's whereabouts. But what has the abbey fish tank got to do with the mystery? And why does Ursus have such an interest in what happens to the silent stonemason?

The Drowned Sword
ISBN 0 19 275365 7

A surprise discovery by Hereward means he's in grave danger! The sword he's found has extraordinary power and there's no way he's letting anyone else near it—not even Gwyneth.

There are prisoners on the run, traitors roaming around the local woods, and talk of treason is running rife—the very throne of England is threatened and it may be that Hereward holds the key to it all.

Ursus and Gwyneth must make Hereward see that the treasured sword has to be returned to its burial place—until the time is right for it to be found again . . .